A Crock of Schnitzel

A Komödie by
Barbara Pease Weber

D1047691

Baker's Plays
c/o **Samuel French, Inc.**
45 West 25th Street
New York, NY 10010
bakersplays.com

MUSIC USE NOTE

A CROCK OF SCHNITZEL was featured in the McLaren Comedy Festival in Midland, Texas in August 2010 and thereafter premiered in September 2010 in conjunction with the Philadelphia Live Arts/Fringe Festival in the Barthelmes Auditorium at The German Society of Pennsylvania with the following cast:

TANTE GERTIE/SISTER MARY GERTRUDE . . . . Susan Triggiani

TANTE HILDE/MRS. TOMASSO . . . . Theresa Fries Bateman

MR. TOMASELLI/MR. TOMASSO . . . . Jim Golden

GREG WAGNER/KLAUS WAGNER . . . . Nathan Foley

ASHLEY WAGNER/INGRID WAGNER . . . . Rachel Buck

CHARACTERS

(In Order of Appearance)

TANTE GERTRUDE - Greg's Bavarian busybody of an Auntie

(Gertie's bark is worse than her bite.)

TANTE HILDEGARD - Gertie's sister and Greg's other Auntie

(She won't let you leave hungry!)

MR. TOMASELLI - The Postman

(He gets more than he delivers!)

GREGORY WAGNER - Hilde and Gertie's beloved nephew

(Except for that one time involving Gertie's brassiere on display at the science fair...)

ASHLEY WAGNER - Greg's beautiful new bride

(Watch out for the wormhole!)

INGRID* - Greg's Mother

(Or...is she?)

MR. TOMASSO* - Ingrid's landlord

(Get that rent check ready!)

MRS. TOMASSO* - Ingrid's landlady

(What the heck did she put in those meatballs?)

SISTER MARY GERTRUDE* - A She-Devil

(in a Nun's habit)

KLAUS* - Greg's father

(A fait accompli)

*Roles of Ingrid, Klaus, Mr. and Mrs. Tomasso and Sister Mary Gertrude are to be performed by the same actors who portray Ashley, Greg, Gertie, Hilde and Mr. Tomaselli.

For John, in celebration of 30 fun years of Schnitzel…er…that is…marriage.
Happy 30th Anniversary!
XOXO
Barbara

ACT 1

Scene 1

*(Setting: The one bedroom apartment of newlyweds Ashley and Gregory Wagner located on the top floor of an old Victorian home of **GREG**'s two overprotective and slightly meddling spinster aunts, **HILDEGARD** and **GERTRUDE**.)*

*(At Rise: **HILDE** (pronounced Hilda) and **GERTIE** are readying the apartment for the arrival of the newlyweds.)*

GERTIE. *(holding a feather duster and fiddling with the remote control to the television)* I can't get this to work. *(no response from **HILDE**)* Hilde, how do you work this thing? Hilde! I broke the clicker. Hildegard!

(sound of toilet flushing)

HILDE. *(offstage)* Give me a minute. Get a grip, Gertie. *(entering with bucket carrying cleaning supplies)* Put that down. You shouldn't be fiddling with Gregory's television. It's high tech.

GERTIE. I wanted to watch my program, is all. I clean better with the television on.

HILDE. Bathroom is finished. Put this away for me. I have to rest my knees. *(**GERTIE** takes the bucket and supplies and puts them in the hall closet. **HILDE** flops on the sofa and puts her legs up. **GERTIE** comes back, sits next to her, takes off **HILDE**'s shoes and starts to rub her feet.)* Ahhh. Just do that for a minute. Right there. Ahhhh. Then we'll go downstairs and you can watch your program while I keep an eye on the schnitzel. It's almost finished.

GERTIE. Do you think *the girl* likes schnitzel?

HILDE. Who doesn't like schnitzel?

GERTIE. I don't know. I wonder if *the girl* does.

HILDE. Why wouldn't she like schnitzel? What's wrong with schnitzel?

GERTIE. Maybe she's one of those *vegetariers!*

HILDE. You think she's a brussel sprout?

GERTIE. You never know. She might be. One of those tofu eating *vegetariers.*

HILDE. No. Gregory would have told me. When he called to say they were coming home. I told him that I would make schnitzel. "Nobody makes schnitzel like Tante Hilde," he said.

GERTIE. I bet he married himself a skinny *vegetarier.* Just to spite us.

HILDE. Well, we'll soon find out. They're due home in less than an hour.

GERTIE. We don't know her at all, you know. *The girl.*

HILDE. Her name is Ashley. Not *the girl.* And, you better be nice to her. *(No response from* **GERTIE**. *After a beat)* You hear me, Gertie? You be nice to Gregory's new wife. *Ashley.*

GERTIE. Of course I'll be nice to her. I'm nice to everyone.

HILDE. You are not.

GERTIE. I am so.

HILDE. You're not nice to the postman, Mr. Tomaselli.

GERTIE. Why should I be nice to Mr. Tomaselli, the postman?

HILDE. Because Mr. Tomaselli delivers our mail each day.

GERTIE. Why should I be nice to someone who only brings me bills to pay? Never a check! If Mr. Tomaselli brought me a check once in a while, I would be nice to him.

HILDE. You're always impolite to the stocky teller at the bank.

GERTIE. Why should I be polite to the stocky teller at the bank? She only takes my money. Never gives me any of hers.

HILDE. You're disrespectful to Mr. Polansky, next door.

GERTIE. Why should I show respect to Mr. Polansky, next door? His dog dug up my tomato plant!

HILDE. *(scolding)* You're not nice to anybody, Gertie. But, I'm warning you. You *better* be nice to Ashley. She's Gregory's wife now. And, our new niece.

GERTIE. Not by blood. If she was my niece by blood, I would be nice to her. *(beat)* Maybe.

HILDE. That doesn't matter. If she is good enough to be our only nephew's wife, she is good enough for us. And, you *better* be nice.

GERTIE. I'm also angry with Gregory. I've never been upset with Gregory about anything. Until now. *(beat)* Except that time he used my good brassiere for his seventh grade science project.

HILDE. I remember! He used it to simulate the twin peaks of the Colima volcanoes in Mexico.

GERTIE. But did he have to simulate the Mexican peaks with my good German brassiere?

HILDE. Didn't his project win first place in the competition?

GERTIE. Yes, it did. Thanks to the German engineering of my *büstenhalter*. Which, by the way, was ruined after the volcanic eruptions. I learned to lock up all of my *unter kliedung* around science fair time after that.

HILDE. Oh, what a precious boy he was.

GERTIE. And precocious!

HILDE. That too.

GERTIE. He should not have eloped!

HILDE. What's wrong with eloping? Young couples have been eloping for hundreds of years.

GERTIE. *(feelings hurt)* Wouldn't you have loved to see young Gregory get married?

HILDE. Of course. But…

GERTIE. *(cutting her off)* I think he was very selfish to elope. I bet it was the girl's idea. Gregory would have never shut his only *tanten* out of his wedding day.

HILDE. He didn't really elope, Gertie. He invited us to the wedding. We didn't go, remember?

GERTIE. *(***GERTIE** *flaps her arms as if they were bird wings and pretends to fly around the room like a hawk.)* Did we grow wings, Hildegard? Are we *birds?*

HILDE. No. We are not birds, Gertrude. We do not have wings. But, perhaps we could have…

GERTIE. *(Cutting her off,* **GERTIE** *abruptly changes from a bird into a fish and pretends to swim around the room moving her "gills" and moving her mouth like a fish)* Are we *fish,* Hildegard? Did we grow *gills?*

HILDE. No, Gertrude. We do not have gills. We are not fish. But we *are* Gregory's tanten! Maybe we could have… made an exception. Maybe we could have, you know, gone to Dr. Wolfe and gotten a prescription for something to calm our…

GERTIE. Out of the question! Never again! Have you forgotten…

HILDE. Of course not. I have not forgotten, Gertie. I still have nightmares.

GERTIE. Gregory should know by now how I – how we *both* feel. His wedding should have been here. So that we could witness him make the biggest mistake of his life. In person. Not watch him do it on a DVD.

HILDE. We can have a small party for them here and invite Gregory's friends. They can renew their vows and…

GERTIE. Their vows need renewing already?

HILDE. Probably not. But, that way we get to watch the ceremony. In person.

GERTIE. What if we don't like…*the girl?*

HILDE. *Ashley! Ashley!* I am sure that we will like our new niece, *Ashley!*

GERTIE. I bet *the girl* pushed Gregory into it.

HILDE. Impossible. Gregory is too stubborn. Just like his father. Nobody can push Gregory into doing anything. Or, prod him *out* of doing anything when his mind is made up.

GERTIE. But…what if she's…? Do you think she may be…? *(sheepishly in a stage whisper even though there is no one else around)* You know….she might have a *brötchen in ofen?* *(She guestures as if to suggest a bun-in-the oven [pregnant belly])*

HILDE. Even if Gregory and Ashley *are* baking a *brötchen in ofen*, it's not *our* business. Our nephew is all grown up now. His life is his own.

GERTIE. Gregory is still a boy.

HILDE. Gregory is hardly a boy anymore! He is now a married man. I don't want us to turn into two meddling old Tanten.

GERTIE. But, that is what we are!

HILDE. I know. But it is different now. Gregory has a *wife.*

GERTIE. Gregory will always be my wee wunderkind. Our wee wunderkind.

HILDE. You are right. He will. And one day we'll have a wee- wee-wunderkind to overprotect and spoil. *(**HILDE** motions as if rocking a baby in her arms. She then crosses to the end table and takes a framed photograph of Greg's parents and talks to it.)* Your sisters did good, Klaus. We took good care of your boy. He's all grown up, now. A married man. You and Ingrid would be so proud.

TOMASELLI. *(calling offstage)* Fräuleins Wagner! Is that schnitzel I smell?

HILDE. Mr. Tomaselli? Is that you?

TOMASELLI. *(offstage)* Where are you?

HILDE. Gregory's apartment. Come on up.

TOMASELLI. There you are! My two favorite Fräuleins. *(entering in uniform carrying package)* Mmmmmmmm. I smelled your heavenly Bavarian cooking all the way on Elm Street. Am I in time for lunch?

GERTIE. Depends. What did you bring us today? More bills! Like always!

TOMASELLI. I left *your* mail down in the vestibule. I have a package for *Gregory.*

GERTIE. I'll take it. *(she goes for the package but* **TOMASELLI** *won't give it up.)*

TOMASELLI. Hold on now. *(He turns to* **HILDE.***)* I'll trade *you* the package for a taste of what's cooking.

GERTIE. That's mail fraud. I'll report you to the Post Master!

TOMASELLI. No, it's not mail fraud.

GERTIE. Then it's blackmail!

TOMASELLI. Nope. It's not blackmail either.

GERTIE. Then it's mailnapping. And, I'm going to report you to the Postmaster unless you give me that box.

TOMASELLI. *(imploring to* **HILDE***)* Just one little taste? Please Hilde? Before your wicked sister has me put into a stockade in the center of town for schnitzel envy.

HILDE. I have a plate just for you, downstairs, Mr. Tomaselli. We made that tray for the newlyweds. *(**HILDE** points to a covered tray on the dinette table which she proceeds to take into the kitchen and put in the freezer.)* So they would have a good meal in their freezer for later.

GERTIE. It's for Gregory and *the girl.*

HILDE. She means, Gregory and his new bride, *Ashley.*

TOMASELLI. Are they back? Here? In town?

HILDE. They will be. Any minute now.

TOMASELLI. Gregory got hitched in the Caribbean, didn't he?

HILDE. St. Thomas.

TOMASELLI. Very nice. The Virgin Islands.

GERTIE. Hrrumph. *Virgin* Islands, my foot. You can look high and low and you won't find a *jungfrau* on any of them.

TOMASELLI. Oh, that's right. Now I remember the post card he sent you.

GERTIE. You're supposed to deliver our mail. Not read it!

TOMASELLI. It was a post card!

HILDE. Now, Gertie. Behave yourself. They'll be here any minute.

TOMASELLI. Why did Gregory get married in St. Thomas?

GERTIE. That's what I would like to know!

HILDE. Gregory was working in St. Thomas on his research project. You know he is getting his graduate degree in marine biology.

GERTIE. *Dummkopf!* Gregory of all people should *know* better.

TOMASELLI. About what?

GERTIE. As a marine biologist, Gregory should know that with all the fish in the sea, he shouldn't go marrying the first tuna that hops into his net!

TOMASELLI. Where should I put this?

GERTIE. Let me have it! (**GERTIE** *forcefully grabs the box away from* **MR. TOMASELLI**)

HILDE. Are you on your lunch break, Mr. Tomaselli?

TOMASELLI. Indeed I am, Fräulein Wagner.

HILDE. Would you care to stay to lunch with us?

TOMASELLI. Why, that's very kind of you. If it is no trouble, that is.

HILDE. No trouble at all. You go on ahead and help yourself to a glass of fresh lemonade. There's a pitcher in the icebox. We'll be down in a minute.

TOMASELLI. You are, by far, my most hospitable customer. Not to mention the best cook in the neighborhood.

GERTIE. Oh really? What about the Widow Limberg over on Sycamore?

TOMASELLI. What about her?

GERTIE. I bumped into her down at the market the day before yesterday. Her shopping cart was full of flour, sugar, butter and all sorts of confections. She's baking up a storm it seems. Any idea for whom?

TOMASELLI. Ah, yes. The Widow Limberg on Sycamore. Yes, the kind woman sets aside a cookie or two for me every now and again. I am especially fond of her lady fingers.

GERTIE. I daresay! Hear that, Hilde? Mr. Tomaselli is fond of the Lady Limberg's fingers. *(She wiggles her fingers it the air as if to suggest...who knows what?)*

TOMASELLI. Now, I'm not one to stir the rumor pot. But, I hear from Mrs. Limberg's landscaper that she's been having quite a few problems with her garbage disposal of late requiring repeated service calls from the plumber McCauley.

GERTIE. So, then! Mrs. Limberg is a Girl Scout is she? Scattering her cookies across the neighborhood to gentlemen of service?

HILDE. Don't pay her any mind, Mr. Tomaselli. Go on down and pour yourself a lemonade. We'll be right along and I'll fix you a plate of schnitzel.

(TOMASELLI exits)

Gertie! Where are your manners? What are you insinuating? Now, that's quite enough.

GERTIE. I'm warning you about him, Hilde. He's got an eye for something that doesn't involve delivering the mail. Bills or no bills.

HILDE. *(pointing to box)* What is that? Do you suppose someone sent Gregory and Ashley a wedding gift?

GERTIE. Seems so.

HILDE. Well, who is it from? *(She goes to the package and* **GERTIE** *turns away from her, blocking her from the package.)*

GERTIE. Just somebody.

HILDE. Who? Let me see.

GERTIE. It's none of your business...

(HILDE grabs the box)

HILDE. *(reading label)* The Bavarian Clock Shoppe. Dusseldorf. Someone sent them a clock? From Germany?

GERTIE. Seems so.

HILDE. I wonder who?

GERTIE. Me.

HILDE. You?

GERTIE. Are you hard of hearing? I just said I did.

HILDE. You bought Gregory a clock from Germany? A cuckoo clock? As a wedding gift?

GERTIE. Well.....not exactly.

HILDE. Gertie! You old softie. You do have a heart buried in that cast iron bosom of yours somewhere, now don't you?

GERTIE. I didn't *buy* Gregory a clock.

HILDE. Then what's that in the box?

GERTIE. A clock.

HILDE. Is this your idea of a riddle? If you didn't *buy* Gregory a clock, then how can a clock be in the box?

GERTIE. I didn't *buy* a clock. I'm *giving* Gregory a clock. I sent it away to have it repaired. It's so old. I had to send it overseas. I wanted to send it to the same clock-maker that sold it to Opa.

HILDE. You mean, it is grandfather's cuckoo clock? Opa's clock?

GERTIE. Yes.

HILDE. The same clock that Papa sent to Klaus and Ingrid for a wedding gift? With Papa's blessing that all of their time together as husband and wife be filled joy and happiness!

GERTIE. I thought it would make a nice wedding gift for Gregory. A family heirloom. But, it was broken. So, I had it fixed.

HILDE. It broke because you smashed it.

GERTIE. *(defensively)* I *know*.

HILDE. You smashed the cuckoo clock to pieces.

GERTIE. *(angry at the unnecessary reminder)* I *remember*.

HILDE. You had been drinking.

GERTIE. *(escalating anger)* I *know!*

HILDE. You were completely drunk the evening you smashed Opa's clock.

GERTIE. *(trying to shut her up)* I *REMEMBER!*

HILDE. That was the day that you finally realized….the day that it all sunk in. That Klaus and Ingrid would never again hold their child…

GERTIE. *(cuts her off abruptly)* I *REMEMBER! (beat)* How could I ever possibly forget, Hilde? It changed my life. *Our* lives. *Forever.*

HILDE. Then, why…??

GERTIE. *(Regaining composure but becoming emphatic as her monologue progresses.)* Because I now know that I was wrong to smash Opa's clock. Opa's clock was a family heirloom. Papa wanted Klaus to have it as a wedding gift. To keep it in the family. Oh Hilde, I smashed the clock because I wanted time to stop. We were here. You had just put Gregory to bed and were getting ready to cry yourself to sleep for the tenth night in a row. You cried a lot in those days. I drank a lot. Yes! I was drunk when the cuckoo bird came out of his house to sing his cheerful greeting. Cuckoo! Cuckoo! I got so angry at him! How dare he cuckoo so cheerfully when the three of us faced such a tragedy. All I wanted to do was push the cuckoo bird back in his nest and turn back the clock. Turn it back to happier times. But, you can not turn back a clock, Hilde. It is impossible to stop time. Instead, I took down the clock and smashed it to pieces. Just to quiet the cheerful cuckoo. As if what had happened was somehow all his fault.

HILDE. Oh, Gertie. Such painful memories.

GERTIE. But, I have realized that there was a reason to be cheerful! After all, you and me and Gregory. We did good, didn't we?

HILDE. Yes we did. We sure did.

GERTIE. Our time all together. It has been precious. Hasn't it?

HILDE. Of course. It has. But, still, I would have traded it all if only…

GERTIE. *(cutting her off)* Shhhh. So, I decided to have the clock fixed for Gregory. Because it was our Opa's clock. And our Papa sent it to our brother to keep it in the family. And now our only nephew should have it as a wedding gift. It should stay in the family. So, I sent it back to Germany to see if the clockmaker could fix it.

HILDE. And, did he?

GERTIE. He told me he would try. He had trouble trying to locate some of the old parts.

HILDE. Shall we open it? And see?

TOMASELLI. *(from offstage)* Fräuleins! Are you coming down?

GERTIE. Hold your horses old man!

TOMASELLI. My lunch break is almost over. My stomach is grumbling for schnitzel.

HILDE. Here we come, Mr. Tomaselli. **(GERTIE** *and* **HILDE** *exit arguing as sisters do.)* I also have a gift for Gregory.

GERTIE. What? What did you buy for him?

HILDE. I didn't say I *bought* a gift, I said I *have* a gift….. An heirloom. It was Oma's.

GERTIE. Oma's! Hilde! You are such a copycat! *(she closes door to apartment)*

HILDE. *(offstage, fading)* I am *not*.

GERTIE. *(offstage fading)* Yes! You are! Just because I am giving Gregory something that belonged to Opa, you are giving something that used to be Oma's!

HILDE. That is not the reason.

GERTIE. Is so!

HILDE. Is not!

(A moment or two after the aunts exit to their down-stairs apartment, the opposite side/kitchen door opens and **GREGORY** *and* **ASHLEY** *enter groping and kissing in supercharged honeymoon hormonal overdrive. After several moments of a kissing and groping frenzy that is "just a little PG" but definitely not too over the top for audiences,* **GREGORY** *pulls away, stops and sniffs the air a few times. Then, after a beat, he gleefully proclaims directly to the audience.)*

GREG. SCHNITZEL!

ASHLEY. What?

GREG. I smell schnitzel!

ASHLEY. Schnitzel?

GREG. Yes! Can't you smell it?

ASHLEY. *(Ashley, confused, checks the bottom of her shoes.)* Maybe I stepped in something.

GREG. *(laughing)* No! Not shitzel! *Schnitzel!*

ASHLEY. Is that...a good thing?

GREG. Oh, yeah! It's a wonderful thing. It means the tanten are not angry with me after all. Or, at least they're not very angry, that is. I know they're both a bit miffed.

ASHLEY. As well they should be. I bet they hate me!

GREG. Never! They'll love you. But, not as much as I do. *(He attacks her neck again with kisses.)*

ASHLEY. *(pushing him away)* I doubt it. Your aunts probably think I pushed you into getting married in St. Thomas. If they only knew!

GREG. *(nuzzling her neck)* Does this look like you pushed me into it?

ASHLEY. They probably think that I'm pregnant and I made you marry me. That I forced you into a corner.

GREG. *(now nuzzling the opposite side of her neck as he puts his arms around her waist and backs up, pulling her with him into a corner)* Help! Somebody help! I'm forced into a corner and I can't get out.

ASHLEY. *(breaking away)* Would you be serious!

GREG. Relax. The aunts will adore you. I know they are not angry because I can smell schnitzel cooking downstairs! My favorite food since I was a little boy. Call it my Tanten German comfort food.

ASHLEY. Tante, that's German for Aunt, right?

GREG. Yes. Tante Hildegard and Tante Gertrude. Two peas in a pod. They are not only my aunts, but took on the role of my mother, my father, my grandparents, homework helpers, baseball coaches and well, you name it, they did it all.

ASHLEY. You must love them very much.

GREG. As much as I love you. *(going for her neck again, then after a beat:)* But, don't worry, in a much *different* way.

ASHLEY. Did you ever miss not having parents when you were growing up?

GREG. Oh, sure. But, they died when I was a baby and I really don't remember them except for old photographs and all of the stories that the tanten told me over the years. And, some of those stories...I think they are half fact and 75 percent fiction.

ASHLEY. A boating accident. Of all things.

GREG. That's right. Off the coast of Cape May.

ASHLEY. That's so...tragic.

GREG. It was. My father and mother were celebrating their second wedding anniversary.

ASHLEY. That's even worse. They were practically newly-weds.

GREG. They met when my father came here from Germany to study biology. My mother was in nursing school. It was love at first sight, my aunts told me. They got married, got a pretty good deal on this house from their landlords. An old Italian couple who wanted to sell the place and eventually move to Florida.

ASHLEY. This house?

GREG. Yes. In fact, this was my parent's apartment. They rented it for a while then bought the place from their landlords who then became my parents' tenants. To surprise my mother on their second anniversary, my father chartered a small boat so they could do some fishing and sight-seeing along the coast. The weather turned and - who knows. I guess my father wasn't quite the sailor he thought he was. Or maybe the boat wasn't seaworthy. No one really knows what happened. The Coast Guard located the boat a few days later. It was pretty torn up. My parents were never found.

ASHLEY. Thank goodness you weren't with them!

GREG. The aunts told me that the old couple, the people who they bought the house from, lived downstairs, where the aunts live now. They watched me for the weekend. They were the ones who called my father's family in Germany to tell them about the accident. I stayed with them until my aunts arrived.

ASHLEY. And your aunts came here from Germany to care for you?

GREG. Well, that's a whole other story. My father was the aunts' younger brother. After the accident, they flew over to meet with the Coast Guard and take care of my parents' personal effects, and ultimately me to take me back to Germany with them. But their flight over, to hear the tanten tell it, well it was a pretty rough ride.

ASHLEY. Why?

GREG. One of the engines caught fire half way across the Atlantic and there were all kinds of electrical problems. Of course, there was also the requisite lightning storm and the plane pretty much bounced its way across the ocean on the remaining engine like a beach ball. The tanten were sure they were going crash and wind up in the sea with my parents. And, since it was right after my parents' accident, the aunts vowed to never ride in an airplane or get on a boat anywhere, ever again.

ASHLEY. I can't say as though I blame them.

GREG. So, they were stuck here in New Jersey because they wouldn't fly or sail and, of course, they couldn't walk back home to Germany. Instead, they stayed here, became citizens, and raised me right here in this house which my parents purchased from the old Italian couple shortly before the accident.

ASHLEY. Yet, after all that, your aunts didn't pass any of their fears of flying or sailing onto you. Amazing.

GREG. I think they're full of German superstition. I fly. I sail. I've conquered some pretty wild roller coasters in my teens. Don't tell the aunts, but I even bungee jumped a couple of times. The aunts say I do it to prematurely age them so they die from worry and I inherit their vast estate. *(He holds his arms out as if to suggest "all this" and shrugs.)* I just...I just don't want to stop living out of fear. *(nuzzling again)* And besides, if I didn't fly...and...if I didn't sail...and if I didn't wind up in St.Thomas... I wouldn't have met you, and...we wouldn't be having this conversation, and... we wouldn't have had all the great sex. *(He grabs her, she shrieks with glee, they fall into the sofa kissing and clawing. After a second or two we hear* **HILDE** *outside the door that leads from the newlyweds' apartment to the main part of the house where the aunts live.* **GERTIE** *and* **TOMASELLI** *are behind her.)*

HILDE. *(outside of door)* Hello? Gregory? Ashley? Is that you?

(The newlyweds are too busy getting down to business to hear her initially. Then **GERTIE** *pushes* **HILDE** *aside and opens door and barges in to find* **ASHLEY** *and* **GREG** *"at it" on the sofa.)*

GERTIE. *(hands on her hips)* Ach du lieber! They're not here for *zehn minuten* and they're already *beischlafen* on the sofa.

*(***ASHLEY** *is naturally embarrassed by the "first impression" and jumps up and straightens her clothing and hair.* **GREG** *also jumps up, does not care a lick about his disheveled appearance and runs to his aunts.)*

GREG. Tanten! I missed you! It's great to be home! *(***GREG** *picks up* **GERTIE** *off the ground and swings her around.)* Tante Gertie! What have you done to your hair? You look like a young girl!

GERTIE. *Meine Gute!* You're just trying to butter me up because you know I'm angry with you!

GREG. You can never stay angry with me, Tante Gertie! You know that! *(He kisses* **GERTIE** *on her cheek.)* Tante Hilde! *(He circles her studiously.)* Have you lost weight? You have! You look great! *(He kisses* **HILDE** *on the cheek.)* Don't get too skinny now!

HILDE. Oh! Gregory! How good of you to notice! I've been trying to follow Weight Watchers.

GERTIE. Yes. She watches her weight rise on the scale with each strusel she bakes.   ·

(Note: If the actor portraying **GERTIE** *is heavier than the actor playing* **HILDE,** *she may choose to say instead: "Yes. She watches* my *weight rise on the scale with each strusel she bakes.")*

TOMASELLI. Hello Gregory. Remember me?

GREG. Sure I do. *(They shake hands.)* Hello Mr. Tomaselli. Nice to see you again. Still bringing Tante Gerite all those bills she loves to receive each month?

TOMASELLI. Neither rain, nor hail nor sleet nor chill would deter me from bringing Fräulein Gertrude a bill! I am convinced that your Aunt Gertie would be utterly miserable unless she always had something about which to complain.

GREG. *(laughs)* Then, I'd say you know my Aunt Gertie pretty well, Mr. Tomaselli.

HILDE. Gregory.

GREG. Yes, Tante Hilde?

HILDE. Aren't you forgetting something – or – should I say some *one? (She points to* **ASHLEY.***)*

GREG. *(laughing)* Forget my new bride? Hardly! *(He goes to* **ASHLEY,** *grabs her hand and pulls her into the commotion.)* Tante Hilde and Tante Gertie, I'd like you to meet my incredibly beautiful, smart, talented and completely wonderful wife, Ashley. Who also happens to be a kind, compassionate and very capable nurse. Ashley, these are my – I guess I should say *our* – Aunts. Hildegard and Gertrude.

ASHLEY. It's wonderful to finally meet you. Greg told me so much about you. You're all he talks about.

HILDE. *(hugging her)* The pleasure is all mine. Welcome to our family. I'm sure Gregory has told you, his dear mother was also a nurse.

ASHLEY. Yes. I know.

HILDE. Did you work as a nurse in St.Thomas?

ASHLEY. Yes. In fact, that's how I met Greg. *(turning to* **GREG***)* Didn't you tell them?

HILDE. Tell us what?

ASHLEY. I had the opportunity to work in a hospital in St. Thomas as part of a nursing exchange program. I worked in the Emergency Room. I met Greg when he came in after he had an accident on the boat.

(The **TANTEN** *overreact in a panic, hug each other and shriek.)*

HILDE. A boat accident! Gregory! No!

GERTIE. History repeats itself! Our family is cursed!

GREG. *(to* **ASHLEY***) That's* the reason I didn't tell them how we met.

ASHLEY. No. I'm so sorry. Not a boat accident. Greg got a fish hook pretty mangled in his thumb and I got it out for him and gave him a tetanus shot. Stitched him up good as new. And, to thank me for my efforts, Greg asked me out for coffee. The rest is pretty much history.

GERTIE. *(giving* **ASHLEY** *the evil eye)* Did Gregory have you sign one of those pre-nuptial thing-a-ma-jigs? *(beat)* For when your marriage fizzles out? Like most marriages do today when young people rush into them like you and Gregory did. You have a less than fifty-fifty chance, you know. According to *People* magazine.

HILDE. Gertrude! Really!

GERTIE. I'm just trying to be realistic. The majority of marriages in this day and age end up in *scheidung.*

HILDE. What's gotten into you?

GERTIE. Well, if they don't have one of those pre-nup things then I'll have to be sure to change my Will around so that *(she points)* you-know-who doesn't somehow inherit the family fortune.

GREG. The family fortune? *(sarcastically)* I forgot to tell you, Ashley, Aunt Geritie was among the height of the aristocracy in Germany. Can't you tell?

ASHLEY. *(Completely taken back by the preposterous question.)* I...I...uh. *(beat – then standing her ground)* No, actually, I did not sign a pre-nuptial agreement. In fact, neither of us signed a pre-nup. We didn't feel as though such a legal instrument was...either necessary – or appropriate - under the circumstances.

GERTIE. *(to **HILDE**)* See! I was right! There is a *brotchen in ofen!*

GREG. *(Admonishing and stern.)* No, Tante Gertie. You are wrong. I am disappointed that you could even think such a thing. *(Beat. Then **GREG** slyly winks at **GERTIE** and puts his arm around **ASHLEY**.)* Ash and I are way more careful than that.

GERTIE. Bah! Then what *circumstances* is she talking about?

ASHLEY. The circumstances that we both love each other very much and want to spend the rest of our lives together.

GERTIE. *(mocking)* They "love" each other. Humbug. *(to **HILDE**)* I can smell a gold digger a mile away.

GREG. *(scolding playfully)* Tante Gertie, you're still a cantankerous She-Devil, I see. *(to **ASHLEY**)* Don't be afraid of her, Ashley. Her bark is a lot worse than her bite. *(to **GERTIE**)* For your information, Tante Gertie, Ashley is not like my other girlfriends. Remember? The ones you scared away? This one fights back. That's why I married her. *(**GREG** gives **ASHLEY** a kiss.)*

GERTIE. Suit yourselves. I'll call my *anwalt* in the morning.

GREG. You do that, Tante Gertie. You do that. And, by the way, since when do you have a lawyer? You hate lawyers!

GERTIE. Smart alec! *(she hits him playfully on the side of the head)* I'm not so keen on marine biologists these days either. Especially ones who deprive their aunties of the joy of seeing them get married.

HILDE. Don't pay attention to her, Ashley. Gertrude suffers from post-menopausal moodiness. From too many years of *schlichtheit.*

GERTIE. Speak for yourself. What do I look like? A *Nun?* Ha! *(She gyrates her hips.)* I've had plenty more *beischlafen* than you have over the years.

HILDE. My foot you have.

TOMASELLI. *(clears his throat)* Fräuleins! This conversation contains entirely too much information for my delicate ears. I must get back to my postal duties. It is good to see you again, Gregory. Congratulations on your nuptials Fräu Ashley. May your marriage and mail be filled with many blessings and few bills.

ASHLEY. Thank you, Mr. Tomaselli. It was nice to meet you.

*(*TOMASELLI *exits.)*

HILDE. Well, Gert. You've set yourself a new record. You've only known Ashley about five minutes and you already owe her an apology. *(no response from* GERTIE*)* Go on. I'm sure Ashley would graciously accept your apology with no remorse or hard feelings, wouldn't you, Ashley?

ASHLEY. *(thinks)* Well, that depends.

HILDE. On what?

ASHLEY. On how *sincere* Tante Gertie's apology is, of course.

HILDE. You were right, Gregory. Smart girl.

GREG. I told you.

ASHLEY. And, I think I know what Tante Gertie's problem is.

GERTIE. I don't have a problem!

ASHLEY. Oh yes you do. Want to know what it is?

GERTIE. No!

ASHLEY. I'm going to tell you anyway. Your problem is... me.

HILDE. You?

ASHLEY. Yes. Of course. I am Aunt Gertrude's problem. Tante Gertie is completely jealous of me. For no valid reason I should add. Here I am, the new woman in Gregory's life. Oh, there have been others over the years but they weren't threatening to Aunt Gertie. I am the threat. Because I'm here to stay. You see, Tante Gertie is afraid that since Gregory is in love with me that he will have less love to go around for her and for you, Tante Hilde. Tante Gertie is under the false belief that Gregory's love is like *(thinks for a beat)* a zero sum game.

HILDE. *(to* **GREG***)* Is that like Monopoly?

GREG. No. It's like…*(thinks for a quick beat)*… an apple pie. Tante Gertie is afraid that if Ashley eats the last piece there will be none left for her.

HILDE. *(dismissivly)* No, that is silly. I would just bake another one.

ASHLEY. *(excited, turning to* **HILDE***)* Exactly! You understand, Aunt Hilde! *(***HILDE*** smiles proudly but utterly confused as to why she was correct)* Aunt Gertie should not be jealous of me at all. In fact, I'm the one who ought to be jealous of her. And, of you.

HILDE. Why is that?

ASHLEY. Because Gregory has only been in love with me for a relatively short time. But Greg has loved the both of you practically his entire life. Percentage wise, that means that Greg loves both of you about 180%, in the aggregate, more than he loves me. So, you see, Tante Gertie has absolutely nothing to be worried or jealous about. In fact, I hope one day she will grow to like me and maybe even love me like I was her own niece. Greg's love for me in no way diminishes the love he will always have for both of you.

HILDE. *(sniffling into a tissue, holding back tears of joy)* Oh Gregory! You were right. She is absolutely *wunderbar*. *(She goes to Ashely and gives her a great big hug.)* And, so good at arithmetic!

ASHLEY. So, how about it, Tante Gertie? If you offer me a sincere apology, I promise to graciously accept it. Then, we can start fresh. *(She holds out her hand to shake* **GERTIE***'s.)* Deal?

GERTIE. *(head down, embarrassed)* Jawohl. Bitte akzeptieren sie meine entschuldigung. *(She shakes* **ASHLEY***'s hand.)*

GREG. Very good, Tante Gertie. I'm proud of you.

ASHLEY. Well, I guess that's a start. But I was hoping to receive your apology in English. Otherwise, how do I know that you didn't just tell me to go roll in the mud or stick my head in the oven?

GERTIE. *(raising her head and breaking a smile)* I said. "Yes. "Please accept my apology."

HILDE. Gregory, let's go run down to the store and buy a lottery ticket. This must be our lucky day. Gertie just apologized, out loud, for the first time in history! In two languages!

ASHLEY. *(hugging* **GERTIE***)* Thank you. I am happy to accept your sincere apology, Aunt Gertie. And, now I have a favor to ask you.

GERTIE. *Ach du lieber!* I just apologized. Now she wants a favor on top! Don't push your luck, young lady!

ASHLEY. I would like to ask you to teach me to speak German. You'll have to go slow though. I know some French and a little Spanish but I never learned German except a few words from Gregory.

GERTIE. Naughty words?

GREG. What else? I learned them from you!

ASHLEY. So, if it wouldn't be too much trouble, can you teach me to speak German? That way, if you ever do tell me to roll in the mud or stick my head in the oven, I'll know what you're saying.

GERTIE. *Aber ja!* That means, "Yes, of course."

ASHLEY. Wonderful. And, Tante Hilde, I also have a favor to ask of you.

HILDE. Certainly! What is it?

ASHLEY. I would like you to teach me to cook Greg's favorite German food. Greg tells me that you are the best cook in the whole world and, well, I could certainly use some help in that department.

GERTIE. *(sarcastically, to* **GREG***)* You mean to tell us that you didn't marry her for her cooking?

GREG. No. But, Ashley is quite talented in other areas. *(He winks.)*

GERTIE. *Ich bin sicher, sie ist. (sarcastically to* **ASHLEY***)* That means, "I am sure she is."

HILDE. Now, Gertie. You were doing so well. Don't spoil it.

GERTIE. Well…she got me to apologize didn't she? That right there takes some kind of talent.

HILDE. Ashley, it would be my pleasure, that is "*gern geschehen*" to teach you how to cook German. Do you like schnitzel?

ASHLEY. To be honest, I've never had schnitzel. But, I'm anxious to taste it.

HILDE. Well, I hope you are hungry because it's for supper.

GREG. I'm starved!

HILDE. Good! I'm making plenty. I already put a tray in your freezer for later. Come on, Gertie. Let's leave the love birds alone for a while. We'll see you later for supper.

GERTIE. Wait a minute. I want to give them their wedding gift.

GREG. You got us a wedding gift, Tante Gertie?

GERTIE. Of course, I did. Here. Here it is. *(She hands the package to* **ASHLEY***.)*

ASHLEY. Thank you, Tante Gertie. That is very thoughtful of you. May I open it?

GERTIE. Yes. Go on. *Offnen sie das packet.* That means "Open the package."

*(***ASHLEY*** opens the box and takes out the cuckoo clock.)*

ASHLEY. A Bavarian cuckoo clock! It's magnificent!

GREG. Thank you, Tante Gertie. What a surprise.

ASHLEY. Does a little bird really come out and say "Cuckoo?"

GERTIE. It used to. We'll try it and see. That's not just any cuckoo clock. That clock is a family heirloom.

ASHLEY. We will cherish it. I am touched by your thoughtfulness.

GREG. An heirloom? I've never seen it before.

HILDE. That's because it broke when...

GERTIE. *(cutting her off because she does not want to admit to* **GREGORY** *and* **ASHLEY** *why it broke)* ...When it was *dropped* on the floor. By *accident!* I had it repaired because it is one-of-a-kind and it should stay in the family. It belonged to my grandfather, then your grandfather then your father and now you. When your father was a baby, Gregory, he would love to watch the little bird come out of his house and say "Cuckoo." Your father's first word as a baby was "Cuckoo." Hilde and I teased him about it for years. "Cuckoo! Cuckoo!" "Klaus is a little cuckoo!" Your father would get angry and tell our Papa that we were teasing him and we would get into trouble. That didn't last long though. Klaus got even in no time and would put frogs and snails in our beds. Remember, Hilde? What a little *teufelskerl* our Klaus was! *(to* **ASHLEY***)* That means, "little devil of a fellow."

GREG. Well, it's the perfect time to get a new clock.

HILDE. Why is that?

GREG. Because I have an early appointment at the University tomorrow now that I'm finished my research project. I'll need that cuckoo to wake me. Bright and early.

HILDE. Ashley and Gregory, I also have a gift for you. But, it's downstairs. I'll give it to you after supper. I have an idea! After we have our schnitzel we can all play the Apple Pie Game.

GREG. Apple Pie Game?

HILDE. You know. The one you told me about. It sounds like a lot of fun. I'll bake an apple pie and after Ashley eats last piece, I'll bake another one!

GERTIE. *(rolling her eyes) Um Gottes Willen! Meine schwester ist ein idiot! (deadpan to* **ASHLEY***)* That means, "My *schwester* is a *dummkopf.*"

*(***HILDE** *gasps and shoots her a dirty look as the lights quickly fade to black.)*

(Blackout/Curtain)

Scene 2

(The same. Later that evening.)

(At Rise: **ASHLEY** *and* **GREG** *are getting ready for bed.* **GREG** *is in sweat pants and a T-shirt.* **ASHLEY** *is wearing a short strapless nightgown on top of sweat pants. She also wears a flannel shirt, unbuttoned on top which, naturally, spoils some of the effect. Before the lights come up, the cuckoo clock cuckoos loudly eleven times.)*

ASHLEY. *(holding her stomach and groaning in pain)* Oh, my stomach. *(groans)* My stomach.

GREG. What's wrong.

ASHLEY. I ate too much.

GREG. Get used to it.

ASHLEY. You can't possibly tell me they cook like that every day.

GREG. Pretty much.

ASHLEY. How in the world did you grow up in this house and not wind up weighing seven hundred pounds?

GREG. I work out. *(He "makes a muscle" with his arm and strikes a silly Hercules pose.)*

ASHLEY. *(Groaning at either* **GREG** *'s stupid pose or her stomach ache or both)* I'm going to puke.

GREG. I thought you liked the schnitzel.

ASHLEY. That's the whole problem. I think I liked it too much. Now it doesn't seem to like me.

GREG. Want me to see if the drug store is still open? Get something to settle your stomach?

ASHLEY. No. It'll pass. It was that last piece of apple pie that did me in. I should have stopped after the second. But Hilde's homemade whipped cream was so incredible I needed a third slice to sop it all up.

GREG. I warned you.

ASHLEY. Tante Hilde is the only person I've ever met who actually makes her own Halloween candy! It's no wonder there were so many trick-or-treaters at their door tonight. And, Gertie, all dressed up as a she-Devil. Jumping out from behind the door and scaring the little ones like that. *(She laughs.)*

GREG. She's something else, isn't she?

ASHLEY. *(rubbing her stomach and groaning from overeating)* Will you still love me when I'm old and obese? How do you say "get fat" in German?

GREG. *Verfetten. (thinks then playfully)* I can't promise that I'll love you *verfetten.* But the aunties certainly will. You completely won them over after your fourth plate of schnitzel. They seem to think that people with hearty appetites are honest, trustworthy and loyal.

ASHLEY. I feel like a grizzly bear. I just want to curl up and hibernate for six months and sleep off the sixteen thousand calories I consumed today. I'm beat. All that chewing is exhausting. My jaw hurts.

GREG. *(kissing her neck)* You're not too exhausted, I hope.

ASHLEY. I'm resigned to living the rest of my life in sweat pants. I'll never be able to zip my jeans again.

GREG. *(more nuzzling)* Good. Easier access. *(He tickles her.)*

ASHLEY. *(pushing him away)* Hold on there, eager beaver. It's getting late and you have to be bright eyed and bushy tailed for your meeting with the Professor tomorrow, remember?

GREG. We've only been home one day and you're already starting to sound like the aunts. I'm doomed.

ASHLEY. Face it. Three against one aren't good odds.

GREG. Hey. I have an idea. Why don't you come with me? You can explore the town, such as it is, while I'm meeting with Professor Harper. Then, we can meet up for lunch. There's a great little Thai place a couple blocks away.

ASHLEY. Ugh. Don't talk about food. I never want to look at food again. *(beat)* I wonder if there's any pie left? I may be in the mood for a midnight snack.

GREG. You'll feel better in the morning.

ASHLEY. You'll have to roll me out of bed and out the door.

GREG. I'd rather roll you around in bed.

ASHLEY. You can try. But, if I throw up on you, don't say I didn't warn you.

GREG. I'll take my chances.

ASHLEY. What time is your meeting?

GREG. Seven.

ASHLEY. Seven a.m. on a Sunday? That's a pretty unusual time for a research review meeting, isn't it?

GREG. I thought I told you. It's the whole reason we had to be back by today. It's the only time Harper can see me before he leaves the country.

ASHLEY. Where's he going this time?

GREG. Galapagos Islands. He's heading straight to the airport after our meeting.

ASHLEY. Wow. Vacation?

GREG. No. Harper snagged a Consultancy at the Conservatory there. And...I think... *(pause)*

ASHLEY. What?

GREG. I have a feeling...I'm not sure...but I have a funny feeling...

ASHLEY. What?

GREG. I think he may ask me to go with him.

ASHLEY. *Tomorrow?*

GREG. No. No. But, you know, meet him there. To help him on whatever project he's going to be consulting on.

ASHLEY. For pay?

GREG. I would hope so. I may be completely wrong. It's just that he really seemed to like the marine studies I did in St. Thomas and, I don't know...I just have a feeling that's what he wants to see me about. I mean, besides my thesis. I may be getting ahead of myself, but working in the Galapagos is the dream of every marine biologist.

ASHLEY. And what will I be doing, pray tell, when you're gallivanting around in the Galapagos?

GREG. Look, I'm not even sure that's what he's going to ask me tomorrow. But, if he does, naturally I want you to come with me. Unless, of course, you want to stay here and bake pies with the aunties.

ASHLEY. Hmmm. Bake pies with the aunties or travel to the Galapagos with my new husband. Tough choice. I need time to decide.

GREG. No. It's probably not that. I don't want to get my hopes up.

ASHLEY. I know what you mean. Now you've got my hopes up. But, after all I ate today, I doubt I look that great in a bikini so it doesn't matter. I'll be resigned to baking pies with the aunties in sweat pants. *(She groans in pain.)* Oh, my stomach.

(Author's note: "swim suit" may be substituted for "bikini" at the discretion of the director/actor. Not everybody looks that great in a bikini, schnitzel or no schnitzel!)

GREG. Still hurts?

ASHLEY. Not that bad. I just need to concentrate on the pain to keep my mind off daydreaming about of a couple months in the Galapagos.

GREG. Come on. Chase you to the bedroom! We can daydream together. *(He growls and runs for her and she runs screaming and laughing around the apartment with* **GREG** *in hot pursuit.* **ASHLEY** *crashes into the table where the cuckoo clock is and catches it before it falls onto the floor.)*

ASHLEY. See what you made me do! If this broke it would be all *your* fault. But, *who* would your aunt blame for trashing a family heirloom? Not the wunderkind! No, you better believe that I would be the one back on Tante Gertie's *schnitzel list* in no time flat.

GREG. Hey, I just remembered something. We have to change the clocks tonight, don't we?

ASHLEY. Oh! That's right! I completely lost track of what day it is.

GREG. Do we move it up an hour or back an hour?

ASHLEY. Let me think. "Spring forward. Fall back."

GREG. Fall back. So, we set it back an hour.

ASHLEY. Yes. That means you get an extra hour of sleep tomorrow morning. Your appointment with Harper is at seven, but it would otherwise be at eight.

GREG. I'm not going to waste an hour sleeping when I can be doing *other* things. *(He grabs her and she fumbles the clock.)*

ASHLEY. Watch out, will you! This thing is old!

GREG. Let me see it. **(GREG** *takes the clock, looks it over and moves the hour hand one hour back.)* There. We're all set. An extra hour of *playtime!*

ASHLEY. Wait. *(she sees a note affixed to the clock)* Here's a note. I can't read it. It's in German. *(hands note to* **GREG***)* What does it say?

GREG. *(reads note)* It says..."It's time to have a steamy night of *liebeswerben* with your new wife before she turns into a big fat cow. Get moooooving!"

ASHLEY. *(She slaps his arm.)* It does not!

GREG. It says: *(reading slowly)* "Do not re-set the clock. Do not touch the hand dials. The clock is old and very sensitive. Too much handing will result in a negative impact." Oh well. We blew that one, didn't we? **(GREG** *crumples the note and puts it in his pocket.)*

*(***GREG*** carries the clock under one arm as he chases after* **ASHLEY** *who screams tries to evade him by running around the apartment and ultimately into the bedroom, with* **GREG** *in hot pursuit as the lights fade to black. Music is heard. Possibly a German symphony as if to suggest a sexual interlude. Cymbals crash a few times to suggest the big moment(s). More music, perhaps from a German beer hall. Stage lights can flash and flicker*

*a bit to suggest that something is happening. Another
cymbal crash or two because, after all, it's prime time for*
GREG, *then the music fades and the cuckoo clock cuckoos eleven times to suggest it is now mid morning. The
lights come up slowly. There is a knock on the door. It is*
MR. TOMASSO, *the landlord, who, we (and* **ASHLEY***)
recognize has having met as* **MR. TOMASSELLI**, *the mailman, the day before.)*

MR. TOMASSO. *(knocking)* Mrs. Wagner! Are you there? Mrs.
Wagner?

ASHLEY. *(calling from the bedroom)* Just a minute!

MR. TOMASSO. Hello! Mrs. Wagner?

ASHLEY. *(Offstage.)* I'm coming! I'm coming! Owww! *(beat)*
Ohhhhhh. That hurt! Owwww! *(She enters from the bed-
room hopping/limping on one foot and rubbing her head.
She opens door.)* Yes? Oh! Hello Mr. Tomaselli.

MR. TOMASSO. *(sternly correcting her)* Tomasso! Tomasso!
Not Tomaselli!

ASHLEY (AS INGRID). I'm sorry. I thought your name was
Tomaselli. Do you have mail for us?

TOMASSO. Mail for you? Why would I have mail for you?
That's what the Post Office is for! Besides, it is Sunday.
There is no mail delivery on Sunday!

INGRID. *(confused)* Oh. Well, then, what can I do for you
this morning? Would you like a cup of coffee?

TOMASSO. No thank you. I have had my morning coffee.
Hours ago. I've come to collect the rent check. Your
rent is due today. The first of the month.

INGRID. Rent check? I thought Greg's Aunties owned this
house. I thought the house was put in trust for Greg.

TOMASSO. What are you talking about? What Aunties?
Who is Greg?

INGRID. Who is Greg? Greg is Gertie and Hilde's nephew.
Gregory Wagner.

TOMASSO. And, I'll ask again. Who is Gregory Wagner to
you?

INGRID. *(confused)* Why, Mr. Tomasel...*(She catches herself.)* er, Mr. Tomasso....Gregory Wagner is my husband. Don't you remember? We met yesterday, shortly after Gregory and I arrived.

TOMASSO. Are you feeling all right today, my dear?

INGRID. Yes. That is, I just stubbed my toe and banged my head getting to the door because you woke me out of a pretty deep sleep. But, otherwise, I feel fine. Why do you ask, Mr. Tomaselli? *(shakes her head, confused by the name change)* I mean, Mr. Tomasso.

TOMASSO. Because, you keep calling me Mr. Tomaselli. And, because your husband's name is...

MRS. TOMASSO. (**HILDE** *enters as* **MRS. TOMASSO,** *cutting him off midsentence.)* Mrs. Wagner, is your husband at home this morning?

INGRID. Tanta Hilde! Greg left early this morning for a meeting with his Professor. Remember?

MRS. TOMASSO. Greg? Who is Greg? I need to speak with your *husband.* I have a question to ask him.

INGRID. Tante Hilde! Greg is my husband.

MRS. TOMASSO. *(to* **TOMASSO***)* Why does she call me Tante Hilde?

INGRID. What?

MRS. TOMASSO. *(to* **TOMASSO***)* Do you think she could be sick? We should maybe call the doctor.

TOMASSO. She told me she stubbed her toe and bumped her head.

MRS. TOMASSO. That must be it. A knock on the head. She's talking nonsense.

INGRID. No! I'm fine. Tante Hilde, what is going on? Did Tante Gertie put you up to pulling a prank on me because I insisted that she apologize to me yesterday after she made the crack about the pre-nup?

MRS. TOMASSO. Poor child. Come sit down. Where is Klaus? He maybe should take you to the hospital.

INGRID. Klaus? I don't know anyone named Klaus!

TOMASSO. She really must have knocked the sense right out of her. I do hope the baby will be all right.

MRS. TOMASSO. The baby! We better call for an ambulance.

INGRID. The baby? What are you talking about? *What* baby?

TOMASSO. *(to* **MRS. TOMASSO***, shaking his head)* This is *bad. Very* bad.

> *(***GREG** *(as* **KLAUS***) enters from side door dressed in slacks and a jacket and carrying a newspaper. He may have a mustache, glasses and/or wear his hair a bit differently from* **GREG***.)*

KLAUS. *(cheerfully, with German accent)* Good morning Mr. and Mrs. Tomasso. I am glad you stopped by. I have the rent check for you. First of the month. I am pleased to honor my obligations. Like *clockwork!*

INGRID. I didn't know you paid rent. I thought this house belonged to you and your aunts!

KLAUS. Have you forgotten, Ingrid? We always pay the rent the first of every month. And, when we sign the agreement to purchase the property from the Tomassos, the Tomassos will give us credit for rent already paid. Isn't that right, Mr. Tomasso?

TOMASSO. Yes. That is our arrangement, Mr. Wagner.

INGRID. Ingrid? Why did you just call me *Ingrid?*

KLAUS. *(laughing)* What else would I call you… besides *sleepyhead?* It is past eleven o'clock. You slept very late this morning.

INGRID. Did you meet with Professor Harper already? Did he say anything about joining him in the Galapagos?

> *(***KLAUS** *looks at her with confusion.)*

MRS. TOMASSO. She bumped her head. We were about to call for a doctor.

INGRID. I don't need a doctor! What the *hell* is going on around here? Look, I can take a joke just as well as anybody else but this bullpiddle is getting a little stale. Wait a minute. *(to* **KLAUS***, grinning)* Is this a prank for some kind of reality television show? Where's the video camera? *(she looks around)*

MRS. TOMASSO. Oh, my! Such language coming from someone in her condition.

TOMASSO. Very unbecoming. But, she did bang her head. Let's give her the benefit of the doubt.

KLAUS. Ingrid! *Liebchen*, are you all right? What's gotten into you?

INGRID. Would you please stop calling me Ingrid! The joke is over, Greg. I get it. I'm "Prankensteined" or "Video Vultured" or whatever they call it these days. Ha. Ha. L.O.L. You can post it on a web site for all our friends back in St. Thomas to laugh at me.

KLAUS. Ingrid. Please. Let's go to the Emergency Room. Have them check you over.

INGRID. All right. That's enough. You pulled one over on me, Gregster. Nice work Aunt Hilde. You had me fooled all right, Mr. Tomaselli. I think I'll go get changed then head out for a run. Check out the sights in town. Work off those calories from yesterday. My stomach feels absolutely enormous. (*She rubs her slightly protruding belly.*)

(**KLAUS** *and* **MR.** *and* **MRS. TOMASSO** *look worriedly at each other.* **SISTER MARY GERTRUDE** (*formerly known as* **AUNT GERTIE**) *enters the open apartment door.*)

SISTER MARY GERTRUDE. (*To* **ASHLEY**) Ah, there you are, my child. When I didn't see you at mass this morning, I became worried. I thought you may have...well, you know... been blessed with a new *beginning!* But, it is still much too early! I'm so relieved. Are you feeling all right, my dear?

INGRID. You're late to the party, Gertie. Your cronies here really had me going for a couple minutes though. (*pointing to* **SISTER MARY GERTRUDE**'s *nun outfit.*) Hey, great get up you got there. Maybe I can borrow it next Halloween.

SISTER MARY GERTRUDE. What in heaven's name is she going on about?

KLAUS. *(goes to telephone and dials)* Operator, I need an ambulance please. This is an emergency. Yes. I'll hold. Thank you.

MRS. TOMASSO. *(To* **SISTER MARY GERTRUDE***)* Just humor her. It's for the best. *(She gestures that* **ASHLEY** *has hit her head while silently mouthing this to* **SISTER MARY GERTRUDE.***)*

SISTER MARY GERTRUDE. *(Catching on.)* Ah, well then! Of course! Of course! Halloween. *(sarcastically)* You want to borrow my habit to go trick or treating next Halloween! You know, Halloween is not a holiday! The following day, which is today by the way, today is a holiday. A religious Holy Day. Which is why I was concerned when you didn't come to mass today, my dear. *(her demeanor becomes suddenly sinister)* I was worried that your soul and the soul of your unborn child would *rot in hell* for all of eternity for missing the Sacrament! *(she catches tone)* But, of course, I wasn't aware that you had had an *accident.* No. No. You can't be held responsible for having an *accident...(She lets it rip.)* IF that is what it was that you *really had* and you didn't just OVERSLEEP because you were up all night *doing heaven only knows what young couples do when they should be sleeping!* No. No. Halloween is a dreadful pagan day when the children of the world are influenced by evil forces of Satan himself at work! I despise Halloween! Why should I bother to care about the despicable day that all of the neighborhood children bang on the convent door and demand treats from those of us who have sworn a vow of poverty and cannot afford the luxury of confections! No treats! Trick I say! *TRICK!!*

*(***ASHLEY*** *listens to* **SISTER MARY GERTRUDE** *in sheer horror thinking that* **AUNT GERTIE** *has flipped her lid and her mean streak has resurfaced.)*

KLAUS. *(hanging up)* The ambulance will be here in a minute.

SISTER MARY GERTRUDE. *(to* **KLAUS***)* I suppose YOU over-slept too, didn't you Klaus? Is that why *you* were not in church this morning?

KLAUS. You are wrong, Sister Mary Gertrude. I was at church this morning. I attended the six o'clock mass. When, I am certain that YOU were still sleeping as I did not see you in any of the pews. My wife did not sleep well last night as a result of her delicate con-dition. I saw no point in waking her to join me. Of course, I am sure with all of your compassion, you will see fit to understand and forgive a minor transgres-sion. In fact, I am sure that you could help to arrange for my wife to be given the Sacrament at the hospital. We are about to go there now as my wife is suffering from some sort of concussion.

INGRID. For the last time! I do not have a concussion! I am NOT going to the hospital! For Pete's sake, I'm not even Catholic!

*(***SISTER MARY GERTRUDE,*** the* **TOMASSOS** *and* **KLAUS** *all gasp in horror at this religious revelation.)*

What? Why is everyone staring at me?

(An ambulance siren is heard in the background.)

TOMASSO. *(Looks out the window.)* The ambulance has arrived.

MRS. TOMASSO. Thank goodness! We will be sure to say a prayer for Ingrid and for the baby.

KLAUS. Come along, *liebchen.* Let's get your coat on. We don't want the baby to get cold.

INGRID. Why does everybody keep talking about a BABY???? What baby??? There is no baby here!!! Do you see a baby anywhere??? Wait a minute. *(suspiciously)* If they are calling you Klaus. And you are calling me Ingrid. Then…then…*(She looks down at her slightly protruding stomach and touchs it.)* No. That's impossible! This isn't happening. I refuse to believe it! This is absurd! What in the world is going on here? This is ...this is...This is a crock of sh...*(She is about to say "shit" but looks around at the mixed company and instead blurts out.)* Schnitzel!

(Blackout/Curtain)

END OF ACT 1

ACT II

Scene 1

(The same. Later that evening.)

(At Rise: **ASHLEY** *(as* **INGRID***) and* **KLAUS** *have just returned from the hospital emergency room.)*

*(***INGRID** *and* **KLAUS** *enter through the side/kitchen door to their apartment.* **KLAUS** *holds* **INGRID***'s arm to steady her as he fears she has suffered a head injury.)*

KLAUS. Here we are. Now, let me help you back to bed.

INGRID. I...I just want to sit in here for a while. I don't want to go to bed quite yet. I have to think.

KLAUS. Can you remember anything yet?

INGRID. Oh, yes. I remember everything. The trouble is, my memory seems to be completely different from yours. Something very strange has happened. And, I don't know what it is.

KLAUS. Here. Let me hang up your coat. Put your feet up on the sofa. *(***KLAUS** *helps her put her legs up and hangs up her coat.)*

INGRID. What day is today?

KLAUS. Sunday. Don't you remember? Sister Mary Gertrude came to call on you this morning when you did not make it to church.

INGIRD. No, I mean what date?

KLAUS. November first.

INGRID. Sunday, November 1st. Then, yesterday was Saturday. October 31st. Halloween. It was the last Saturday in October.

KLAUS. *(confused as to what she is getting at)* Yes...

INGRID. So that means, last night we changed the clock. Moved it back an hour.

KLAUS. *(still unsure of her train of thought)* Yes.

INGRID. *(excited, looking around for the cuckoo)* Where is it?

KLAUS. Where is what?

INGRID. The clock! *(She jumps up to look for it.)*

KLAUS. Please! Stay calm and rest. Please, *liebchen.*

INGRID. Where is the clock??

KLAUS. I'll get it! *(KLAUS goes into the kitchen and takes the clock off of the wall.)*

INGRID. No! The cuckoo clock!

KLAUS. The cuckoo clock?

INGRID. Your grandfather's clock! Where is it?

KLAUS. The cuckoo clock is in our bedroom. Where it always is.

INGRID. Go get it! *(KLAUS dashes to the bedroom and retrieves the clock.)*

KLAUS. Here it is. Please calm down, Ingrid.

INGRID. I AM CALM!!!!!

KLAUS. All right. All right. Why did you want to see the cuckoo clock?

INGRID. I think that this clock has something to do what-ever is happ - *(She catches herself.)* something to do with my memory.

KLAUS. You are not making any sense, Ingrid.

INGRID. *(examining the clock)* It...it's not working!

KLAUS. No. It needs to be repaired.

INGRID. Well, get it fixed! Don't you see? Don't you see???

KLAUS. See what?

INGRID. The clock! We set it back last night. We set it back an hour. Only...something happened, didn't it? Something terrible happened. The note! Where is the note?

KLAUS. What note? What are you talking about? Ingrid, the cuckoo used to keep us up all night so we disabled it. I think when we did that, we accidentally broke it.

INGRID. Yes! You were not supposed to move the hands. I'm telling you, there was a note! It was written in German. It said something like *(trying to remember)* "Do not touch the hand dials. The clock is sensitive. It will have a negative impact."

KLAUS. Yes, well, apparently it did. We stopped the hands so the cuckoo would stop chirping all the night long so we could get some sleep. I think we broke the clock when we did that.

INGRID. *(gets up and takes the clock)* Where is my iPhone?

KLAUS. Your what?

INGRID. My phone. I need to look up a phone number on the internet.

KLAUS. *(He gives her a curious look.)* Do you want the telephone book?

INGRID. *(looks at him, realizing the time difference)* Oh. The phone book. Yes. Okay.

KLAUS. *(KLAUS gets the phone book from the kitchen and hands it to her.)* Yellow Pages?

INGRID. *(she rolls her eyes in disgust at the thought of having to look up a number the old fashioned way)* Fine. **(ASHLEY** *flips through the pages.)*

KLAUS. What are you looking up? A business?

INGRID. Clock repair.

KLAUS. No, darling. I doubt there would be anyone in that book who would be able to repair this cuckoo clock. Don't you remember? Father sent it to us as a wedding gift. It is very old. I feel terribly guilty for breaking it. We will have to send it back to Germany to have it repaired.

INGRID. To Germany!? How long will that take?

KLAUS. A few weeks? A month? Maybe more. What is the rush? What is so special to you about this clock?

INGRID. I don't know! But, there must be something... magical about it.

KLAUS. Magical? Ingrid, really! You are being silly.

INGRID. Well, that's the only explanation I can think of. I must have...I don't know...somehow gotten sucked into a wormhole. This clock must have a wormhole! *(She examines the clock.)*

KLAUS. A wormhole?

INGRID. Yes! You were a science major weren't you? You've never heard of a wormhole?

KLAUS. Ingrid, I studied biology, not physics. But, yes. I do know what the wormhole theory is. It is the travel through space and time. But, what does that have to do with this old cuckoo clock? And what does it have to do with you?

INGRID. Klaus, if I tell you what I truly believe is going on, I am afraid you won't believe me. I am afraid that you will think I'm hallucinating from hitting my head this morning. But even the doctor said that I did not hit my head that hard. He didn't even find a bruise. Klaus, please say you will believe me. No matter how crazy it sounds to you.

KLAUS. Ingrid...I...*(pause)* of course. Of course, I will believe you.

INGRID. Okay. Do you promise?

KLAUS. Yes. I promise.

INGRID. All right. You better sit down. *(*KLAUS *sits)* First of all. My name is not *Ingrid* Wagner.

KLAUS. It is not?

INGRID. No. My name is *Ashley. Ashley* Wagner.

KLAUS. *(playing along)* Ashley Wagner. Are you *related* to Ingrid Wagner?

INGRID. In fact, yes I am. I am Ingrid Wagner's daughter-in-law.

KLAUS. Daughter-in-law? How old does that make you, Ashley Wagner? And how old does that make Ingrid Wagner? And, who then am I?

INGRID. I'm getting to that. Ashley Wagner is Gregory Wagner's wife. That is, *I* am Gregory Wagner's wife. That means, *you* are Ashley Wagner's father- in-law.

KLAUS. I am a bit confused. Who is...what did you say his name is, Ashley Wagner's husband?

INGRID. Gregory. Gregory Wagner. Ashley's husband. That is, *my* husband. Gregory Wagner is your son.

KLAUS. *(looks at* **INGRID**'s *pregnant stomach)* Gregory Wagner is *our* son? *(points to stomach)* Is that Gregory Wagner? In there?

INGRID. I...I think so. Yes. Wait! No! Gregory Wagner is *your* son, and *Ingrid* Wagner's son.

KLAUS. Our son?

INGRID. No! I am Ashley Wagner! Not Ingrid Wagner. I am not your wife! I am Gregory's wife.

KLAUS. And, Gregory is *my* son but not *your* son?

INGRID. Correct.

KLAUS. Because you are my *son*'s wife. Not *my* wife.

INGRID. Correct.

KLAUS. But, *you* are carrying *my* child in *your* womb?

INGRID. *(scrunches her face)* ARRGGGGHHHH! How can I possibly expect you to understand? I don't even understand!

*(***KLAUS** *takes phone book and goes to the telephone)*

INGRID. What are you doing?

KLAUS. Sweetheart, I am very concerned for your heath. And, I am increasingly concerned for the health of our baby. I think you need to consult a psych- *(He hesitates.)* a specialist.

INGRID. Oh Klaus! You promised!

KLAUS. I know, *Liebchen.* By sometimes concussions can be tricky. You can injure yourself and not even know it and then go into a coma. It's not that I don't believe you. In fact, I believe that YOU believe what you are saying is completely true. But, you have to admit that the whole thing is pretty far fetched. What you are asking me ties right into the age old question "What came first, the chicken or the egg?" You seem to believe that you are not only the *chicken, (He points to* *her stomach.)* but that you are also *married to the egg!* I think it would be wise to take you back to the hospital so that they can keep you overnight. For observation.

INGRID. Klaus, please. I don't want to go back to the hospital. Not tonight. Let me just rest here and maybe everything will work itself out in the morning.

KLAUS. Are you sure? This may be serious.

INGRID. Oh. Yes. I'm sure. *(She lies.)* In fact, I think my memory is starting to come back already.

KLAUS. *(He kisses her head.)* Good. You had me quite worried there for a minute. All that talk about cuckoo clocks, wormholes and in-laws.

INGRID. I'm sorry about that. I guess I read too much science fiction.

KLAUS. You read science fiction? Since when?

INGRID. Oh. *(She lies.)* One of the nurses at work lent me a few of her books. That's all.

KLAUS. Well, please stick to the romance novels next time. *(He rubs her stomach.)* They seem to work out much better for you.

INGRID. Yes, they do. Don't they? Ah, I mean. I will. *(She gets up to go to the bedroom then stops.)* Klaus. How many months am I?

KLAUS. About four months. Have you forgotten that?

INGRID. *(to herself, stage whisper)* Of course. Gregory was born in March.

KLAUS. What was that?

INGRID. No. I didn't forget. The baby is due in March.

KLAUS. Yes. Just in time to welcome in the spring.

INGRID. *(She crosses to the clock and picks it up.)* Klaus, it is such a shame that we accidentally broke this clock. After all, it has been in your family for so many years. It was your grandfather's clock, then you father's clock and now your clock. Wouldn't you want to pass it down to the baby as an heirloom? To keep in the family?

KLAUS. Yes, but I think we have some time. Our child is not even born yet.

INGRID. Yes, I know. But, wouldn't it be wonderful give the clock to our baby on his birthday. The day he arrives in the world.

KLAUS. Or she.

INGRID. She what?

KLAUS. Our child may very well be a girl.

INGRID. Oh, yes. Of course. No matter though. Whether our baby is a boy or girl, I want to present him or her with a family heirloom on the day of birth. Please, Klaus, have the clock repaired as soon as possible? So we have it in perfect working condition for our baby?

KLAUS. Very well, Ingrid. Although I doubt our baby will care one way or the other.

INGRID. You are wrong, Klaus! The baby will love watching the cuckoo! Didn't *you* love watching the cuckoo come out of his house and sing "cuckoo" when you were a boy?

KLAUS. In fact, I did. You're right. I will locate a clock-maker in Germany and send the clock to be repaired tomorrow.

INGRID. Thank you!

KLAUS. *(looking at his watch)* It's past supper time. You must be ravenous. You've hardly eaten a thing today. That's not good for you or the baby. Why don't you take a nice warm bath and get settled in bed. I'll bring you in a supper tray. It won't take long. I just have to warm up the schnitzel!

(**INGRID**'s *eyes get wide and her mouth drops open at the word schnitzel.*)

(*Blackout/Curtain*)

Scene 2

(The same. A Saturday evening. Five months later.)

(ASHLEY (as INGRID) has just returned from the baby shower given by MRS. TOMASSO. She and MRS. TOMASSO carry in boxes of baby gifts to INGRID and KLAUS's apartment. INGRID is full-term. INGRID is carrying an uneaten cake and a large gift box.)

MRS. TOMASSO. Ingrid! You shouldn't be carrying anything in your condition. You sit down. We can manage with these. When the men come in from shoveling they can bring up the cradle and the stroller.

INGRID. Oh, Mrs. Tomasso. I can't thank you enough. It was so kind of you to throw me a baby shower.

MRS. TOMASSO. It's the least I could do. You've been such a wonderful friend, Ingrid. It's such a shame that we're moving to Florida next year. We won't be able to see your baby grow up.

INGRID. I'll be sure to send you pictures.

MRS. TOMASSO. Oh yes! Lots of pictures! Every year! Every holiday! And of course, you can come to visit Mr. Tomasso and me any time you want. Take the baby to Disney World.

(SISTER MARY GERTRUDE enters carrying more boxes of gifts and places them on the table.)

INGRID. *(ASHLEY realizes that, of course this will not be possible because there will be a tragic accident in the near future.)* Oh. Well. I...

MRS. TOMASSO. What? You don't like Florida?

INGRID. *(Recovering.)* Of course, I do. In fact, I wish we could move there with you.

SISTER MARY GERTRUDE. *(To MRS. TOMASSO)* You're *lucky* to be moving to Florida. This weather! Spring is just around the corner and here we are getting another two feet of snow! It's yet another dismal excuse for all of the pagans and hedonists to skip mass tomorrow.

Mark my words. In nine months we'll be seeing a lot of our young parishioners finding themselves in YOUR condition, Ingrid. All due to a snowstorm. *Buy shovels, I say!* Get some good old fashioned *outdoor* exercise. Instead of partaking in indoor gymnastics or whatever you young couples do on Sunday mornings when you should be singing hymns at church!

INGRID. *(laughing)* You may be right about that, Sister. I have a feeling the pews will be a bit empty tomorrow morning. *(looking out the window)* I hope that everyone gets home safely. The street is already snow covered. It's really coming down hard.

MRS. TOMASSO. I know. The weatherman said it is going to snow straight through the night.

INGRID. Will you be all right getting back to the convent, Sister? Perhaps you should leave now, while you can. Or, I can have Klaus drive you.

SISTER MARY GERTRUDE. Don't be ridiculous. It would take more than a little snow storm to keep me from getting to church. *(scolding)* You *young* people. You don't know what a real snow storm is. Why, when I was a girl we had twelve feet of snow! Every week! All winter long! Now, those were the days. And, we managed to get to church. On *time!* Every Sunday!

(**MR. TOMASSO** *enters bundled in coat, hat, scarf, and snow-covered.*)

MR. TOMASSO. Well, now. Is the hen party over already?

MRS. TOMASSO. Yes, thanks to the weather. We didn't even get a chance to cut the cake and have dessert.

(**KLAUS** *enters also in hat, coat, scarf and gloves carrying a package which he places on a table next to the door.*)

KLAUS. Did someone say cake?

INGRID. Yes. Come in and get warm. I'll put some coffee on. *(She gets up and starts for the kitchen.)*

SISTER MARY GERTRUDE. I'll do it. You sit down. You look as though you're ready to burst.

INGRID. I feel fine. Like a hippo. But fine. In fact, for some strange reason I have so much more energy today.

MRS. TOMASSO. I baked an apple pie but nobody ate it. Too worried about getting home in this weather. I'll get it. *(She exits to her living area downstairs.)*

INGRID. Klaus, wait until you see the wonderful baby gifts! We have such amazing and generous neighbors.

SISTER MARY GERTRUDE. What did that cheapskate Mrs. Limberg from Sycamore Street give you?

MR. TOMASSO. Why do you call Mrs. Limberg a cheapskate?

SISTER MARY GERTRUDE. You should see what she puts into the collection plate. It's hardly worth passing the plate to her. *Skip over her I say!* Pass the plate around her. Let everyone see what a cheapskate she is. Father Wohler should only give her half a wafer when she receives communion. That will teach her!

KLAUS. You should not talk of such things, Sister. It is none of our business. Mrs. Limberg's contribution to the church is between her and God.

SISTER MARY GERTRUDE. If everyone was such a cheapskate the church would not have candles for the altar let alone a new roof to keep out the Devil himself.

MR. TOMASSO. Oh Mary Gertrude, you do talk a blue streak. I think you've got a bit of the *Devil* in *you.*

SISTER MARY GERTRUDE. Just because you married my sister, Lorenzo Tomasso, doesn't mean you have the right to impugn my character. I have no Devil in me. However, I know one or two things about you that I bet my sister would like to know…*if* I had the mind to tell her.

MR. TOMASSO. Oh really! Like what?

SISTER MARY GERTRUDE. Exactly what was that Limberg woman doing riding in your car last week?

MR. TOMASSO. I beg your pardon!

SISTER MARY GERTRUDE. Don't you dare try and deny it! I saw you with my own two eyes. Heading straight toward the motel on North Boulevard you were. Laughing up a storm, the two of you. And, what were you eating? Ladyfingers? While driving? Disgraceful! *Two hands on the wheel at all times when a car is in motion!* Where did you get your driver's license? At the five and dime?

MR. TOMASSO. Not that I owe you any explanation whatsoever, you Bavarian busybody, now that you've gone and attacked my integrity in front of this innocent young couple, I'll tell you! Mrs. Limberg's car was in the shop and she needed a ride to meet my WIFE at the shopping center to buy Ingrid a baby gift!

SISTER MARY GERTRUDE. A likely story!

MR.TOMASSO. Well, as long as we're clearing the air, maybe Ingrid and Klaus here ought to know why it is in the first place that *you* became a *nun!*

SISTER MARY GERTRUDE. You wouldn't dare!

MR. TOMASSO. Oh, wouldn't I?

INGRID. *(eager to get dirt on* **SISTER MARY GERTRUDE** *but oh so innocently egging him on)* Why *did* you become a nun, Sister Mary Gertrude? What was your calling?

KLAUS. *(smelling trouble brewing)* Ingrid! Don't!

SISTER MAY GERTRUDE. *(to* **MR. TOMASSO***)* I'm warning you, Lorenzo Tomasso!

MR. TOMASSO. You don't scare me, you miserable religious hypocrite! *(to* **ASHLEY***)* When Sister Slandermouth here was a vixen of sixteen –

SISTER MARY GERTURDE. Stop!

MR. TOMASSO. *(continuing)* – her father caught her in the neightbor's horse barn, covered in hay and not much else, all sprawled out and flat on her...

(**MRS. TOMASSO** *enters in nick of time.*)

MRS. TOMASSO. Here we are! Hot apple pie with home-made whipped cream!

KLAUS. Saved by divine intervention once again, Sister Mary Gertrude! *(to* **MRS. TOMASSO***)* Cut me a big slice, Mrs. T. I'm starved!

MRS. TOMASSO. Coming right up. Are you having any, Ingrid?

INGRID. No, thanks Mrs. T. In fact, I don't want to be rude, but I think I'm going to go lie down for a bit. I do feel a little bit tired all of a sudden. Thank you again. For everything.

MRS. TOMASSO. It was my pleasure, my dear. Now, go get some rest. You only have, what is it, a little over a week to go?

INGRID. According to the doctor, I'm right on schedule. Which is pretty unusual for a first baby. But, pretty unusual is par for the course for me these days. Good night. (**ASHLEY** *gets up and starts to exit but does not leave the room quite yet.*)

SISTER MARY GERTRUDE. Sweet dreams, my dear. *Bless the beasts and children!*

MR. TOMASSO. What the hell does *that* mean?

SISTER MARY GERTRUDE. Please! As if you don't know. Since you fall squarely into *one* of the categories.

MRS. TOMASSO. Mary G., what in heaven's name are you going on about?

SISTER MARY GERTRUDE. That's just like you. Always sticking up for *him.* Just remember, blood is thicker than water.

MRS. TOMASSO. Sit down. Have your pie.

KLAUS. It's very good, Sister. You better have a piece of this delicious apple pie before it's all gone and there's *none left for you.*

(**ASHLEY** *stops in her tracks, turns around at this eerily familiar exchange of dialogue, gives* **KLAUS** *a "you've got to be kidding me" expression.*)

KLAUS. Something wrong?

INGRID. *(despondent)* No, nothing. Good night.

SISTER MARY GETRUDE. I know when I'm not wanted. *(getting her coat)* I'm leaving.

MRS. TOMASSO. Oh M.G., stay the night. It's a blizzard outside! I'll telephone the convent and let them know you're staying with us. On account of the weather.

SISTER MARY GERTRUDE. I'd rather freeze. I'd rather get stuck in a snow drift than spend one single night under his roof.

MR. TOMASSO. What's the problem, Mary Gertrude? Afraid I'll sneak in your room and bite you in the middle of the night? Don't worry. (*He puts his arm around* **MRS. TOMASSO.**) I only have a taste for sweet things. Not sourpussies.

(*Author's note: If the word "sourpussies" is thought to be inappropriate or offensive, it may be changed to "sauerkrauts." "Sourpussies" is actually funny and inoffensive when pronounced with an Italian accent.*)

(**KLAUS** *reacts - "What did he just hear* **MR. TOMASSO** *say???" and he chokes on his pie and needs to take a big drink of water*)

SISTER MARY GERTRUDE. (*Extremely offended an appaled by* **MR. TOMASSO**'s *remark*) Did you hear what he just…

MRS. TOMASSO. Now MG, he didn't mean anything by it. Just a slip of the tongue. (*She whacks* **MR. TOMASSO** *in the back of his head and shoots him a look*)

SISTER MARY GERTRUDE. (*to* **MRS. TOMASSO**) You must be a saint. To put up with the likes of him all these years! I'd rather brave the elements (*She exits in a huff.*)

MRS.TOMASSO. She'll freeze to death. She can't walk all the way to the convent. It's clear across town.

KLAUS. (*jumps up*) I'll drive her.

MRS. TOMASSO. No, you stay here with Ingrid. We'll go. She may be a moody old battle-ax, but she's still my sister. And I love her no matter what. Come on, dear. Get your coat on. Maybe you two can kiss and make up.

MR. TOMASSO. I'd rather eat nails.

MRS. TOMASSO. I'll remember that at breakfast time when you ask for my hot fluffy pancakes. Come along, now. (*She exits.*)

MR. TOMASSO. Good night, Klaus. Oh, don't forget, we move the clocks up tonight. Daylight savings is tomorrow already. We lose an hour of sleep but get an hour extra sunlight.

KLAUS. That's right. Thanks for the reminder. And, thank you again for all you've done for us. To welcome our baby.

MRS. TOMASSO. Lorenzo! Come along! I want to catch up with Sister before she freezes in her tracks and gets hit by a trolley.

MR. TOMASSO. *(to KLAUS, shaking his head)* We should only be so lucky. *(He exits.)*

(KLAUS begins to take the cake plates and cups into the kitchen and straighten up. He may peek into one of the boxes and pull out a cute baby outfit or baby toy. After a few moments, INGRID comes out of the bedroom in a bathrobe.)

KLAUS. Can't sleep?

INGRID. I can't get comfortable. I'll try reading a book. That will put me right out. *(She goes to desk and takes out a book)*

KLAUS. How about a cup of warm milk?

INGRID. I'd rather have a shot and a beer.

KLAUS. After the baby. We'll celebrate.

INGRID. *(half heartedly because ASHLEY can't really get into the celebration aspect of this phenomenon)* Yes. *(She sighs with a lack of excitement.)* Celebrate.

KLAUS. *(with compassion for his pregnant wife)* I know it's hard. But, it's almost over. And, it certainly looks like the baby got some really nice things. *(INGRID grimaces and KLAUS reacts.)* What? You don't like the gifts?

INGRID. The gifts are wonderful. I just have a bit of indigestion, that's all. I must have eaten too much at the baby shower. Mrs. Tomasso made a huge tray of lasagna. It was just a little spicy for me I guess.

KLAUS. Sit down and put your feet up. Your ankles look a little swollen.

INGRID. I feel like if you stuck a pin in me I'd fly around the room like a busted balloon.

(**KLAUS** *sits next to her and puts his arm around her.*)

KLAUS. Are you unhappy, sweetheart? Is it me? Did I do something wrong?

INGRID. No, Klaus, no. You are a perfect husband. *(She daydreams of GREG.)* The apple surely doesn't fall far from the tree.

KLAUS. What do you mean?

INGRID. Oh, nothing. *(covering what she really meant)* I guess your father must have also been a perfect husband to your mother.

KLAUS. My father? Hardly. He constantly drank too much and fought with my mother all of the time. My mother once hit him on the head with a frying pan for coming home drunk!

INGRID. You're kidding!

KLAUS. Yes. I am. My father adored my mother. He still does. He does like his beer though. But, not too much.

INGRID. I'm sure your parents have a perfectly wonderful marriage.

KLAUS. Is it the baby? Are you unhappy about becoming a mother?

INGRID. Oh, Klaus. I'm just so…confused. I'm not at all sure if I am ready for motherhood.

KLAUS. And I am not sure that I am ready to be a father. But *(He touches her stomach.)* here we are. And here is our baby. Almost ready to say hello to the world.

INGRID. It's really happening then, isn't it?

KLAUS. It most certainly is.

INGRID. I'm so frightened.

KLAUS. I suspected that. I will be there with you the whole time. *(He takes her hand.)* Holding your hand. And, whispering "I love you" in your ear.

INGRID. But Klaus, how can I make you understand!?

KLAUS. Understand what?

INGRID. That you don't really love *me*. You love *Ingr-* *(Before she can finish the word "Ingrid" she is overcome with a contraction.)* OHHHHH!!!!!!

KLAUS. What's wrong?

INGRID. My stomach! I knew I shouldn't have eaten two plates of lasagna. And that linguine!

KLAUS. *(gets up and goes to kitchen)* I'll make you a cup of hot tea with peppermint. That may settle your stomach. *(He goes to the kitchen to put on the kettle.)*

INGRID. *(Noticing the package the Klaus had put by the door when he entered from shoveling)* What's that? Did someone mail us a gift?

KLAUS. No. The express delivery truck came while I was shoveling.

INGRID. What is it?

KLAUS. I wanted to surprise you. I meant to hide it. Pretend you didn't see it. It's a present for the baby.

INGRID. *(gets up to get the package)* Too late. I saw it. Now I have to open it.

KLAUS. All right. It doesn't matter. *(jokingly)* The baby will still be surprised even if his mother is an impatient spoilsport.

INGRID. *(gets gift, sits back down on sofa and unwraps it – she is completely overwhelmed)* Oh Klaus. It's the cuckoo clock.

KLAUS. Yes. I had the clockmaker promise to do his best to repair it in time. I told him that I wanted to pass it down to our child on the day of his – or her – birth.

INGRID. OHHHHHH. *(long pain then a minute of heavy breathing to recover)*

KLAUS. Ingrid?

INGRID. I have to use the bathroom. What the heck did she put in those meatballs? I think I have to throw up. *(she hurries into the bathroom)*

KLAUS. *(he talks to her outside the bathroom door which is closed)* Need me to help? *(beat – no response)* Hold your head?

(beat – no response) Ingrid? Are you all right in there? *(a few beats then the door opens)*

INGRID. My water broke!

KLAUS. You mean...it's time?

INGRID. It must be. It must be time. It's time. It's TIME! *(beat, she thinks)* Oh Klaus! That's it! It's TIME! It's TIME! *(She dances around!)* Klaus! You're absolutely right! IT'S TIME!

KLAUS. There you are! You see! You are excited about the birth after all. We'll do it together. I'll be right there with you. You'll be fine. Everything will be fine.

INGRID. No! No, that's not what I meant. I mean...today! Today is daylight savings! Today is the day we move the clock ahead isn't it? We do that tonight, right?

KLAUS. Yes. In fact, I had forgotten. Mr. Tomasso had to remind me.

INGRID. Well then! The cuckoo clock came back just in time! Perfect time!

KLAUS. For the baby's arrival! Shall I bring it with us to the hospital?

INGRID. No! I mean, yes but *(another contraction)* OHHHHHHHH. ARGGGGHHHHH. Oh, that was a big one. *(heavy post contraction breathing)*

KLAUS. I'll call the doctor and tell her we are on the way to the hospital.

INGRID. No! Not yet. We have to turn the hand on the cuckoo clock. Move it ahead!

KLAUS. I can do that later. Right now we need to get to the hospital. *(He goes to phone and picks it up and dials a number on a pad of paper next to the phone.)* Hello? This is Klaus Wagner. Is this Dr. Park's answering service? Good. My wife is in labor. Can you please leave a message that Ingrid Wagner is going to the hospital and she should please meet us there? We're on our way now. Thank you. *(hangs up)*

INGRID. *(takes his hand)* Klaus...do you love me?

KLAUS. Of course I do. More than anything.

INGRID. Would you do anything for me? For the baby?

KLAUS. Anything in the world. Anything in my power and within the law or even if I had to break the law.

INGRID. I'm glad to hear you say that, Klaus. Because, what I am about to do is break the law.

KLAUS. Ingrid, what…??

INGRID. I am about to…I HAVE to…break the law of physics.

KLAUS. What are you talking about?

INGRID. Klaus, I know you did not believe me before. But, what I told you was the truth.

KLAUS. What did you tell me?

INGRID. ARRGHH *(holding back a contration or at least trying to)* OOhhhh.. Klaus, what I am saying is, I want Ingrid to experience the joy of giving birth to this baby, not me. I am NOT Ingrid Wagner! I am Ashley Wagner!

KLAUS. Oh, no, Ingrid. Not again!

INGRID. Klaus! I am telling you the truth. And, to prove it, I must move the hand on that clock one hour ahead. Right now. So that Ingrid can give birth to her baby boy, not me.

KLAUS. But, if you touch the parts the clock is apt to break again. And, I just had it fixed. For our baby.

INGRID. If it breaks, it can be repaired again. Or, we can leave it broken. I don't care! If I am wrong, I promise you I will go to see a psychiatrist. You can commit me. You can lock me up in a crazy house and throw away the key. *(another contraction, harder and longer)* OHHHHHHH. ARRRRRRRRR. UGGGHHHHHHH. *(breathing)* Klaus – we're wasting time. The baby is coming. The baby is coming fast. I need to turn the hand on the clock! Right now!

KLAUS. *(frustrated and angry)* Here! Turn it! Burn it! I don't care what you do with it. We've got to get you to the hospital and you're fiddling around the cuckoo clock. I'm going to clear the snow off the car. Or else we won't get anywhere. *(he gives her the clock)*

INGRID. Thank you. Klaus, thank you.

(*KLAUS exits shaking his head in disappointment.* **INGRID** *turns the dial and waits. Nothing happens. She sighs, shakes her head and goes to the bedroom to get her suitcase which is pre-packed for the hospital. She puts on a pair of sweat pants under the bathrobe (the same sweat pants that* **ASHLEY** *wore earlier), returns, puts on her coat, scarf or hat and boots. During this time there is a sound effect of a car trying to start but not kicking over. She sits and waits for* **KLAUS** *to return to get her. After a moment, he returns in a dither.*)

KLAUS. The car won't start!

INGRID. What?

KLAUS. Dead battery!

INGRID. Call an ambulance!

KLAUS. (*rushes to phone and dials 911*) Operator! This is an emergency! My wife is in labor. We need an ambulance to 777 Pendulum Lane...What? No ambulance service tonight? The roads are too icy? But...my wife is in labor! We're going to have A BABY!!!!! Send someone! Please. Well then...do you have any phone numbers for doctors in the neighborhood? (*beat*) Dentists? Thank you. Yes, our phone number is 555-3892. Thank you.

INGRID. OWWWWWWWWWWOOOOOOHHHHHHHH!!!! (*wicked contraction!*) It's coming! (*heavy breathing*) It's coming! (*more heavy breathing*)

KLAUS. Now?

INGRID. Yes, I have to push!

KLAUS. Don't push! Please! Not yet! No pushing!

INGRID. I have to!

KLAUS. Why? Why?

INGRID. I DON'T KNOW! I JUST HAVE TO!!!!!!

KLAUS. Okay! Okay! Lie down. Lie down on the floor. I'll get sheets!

(He helps **ASHLEY** *to lie on the floor then he dashes into the bedroom, grabs two sheets, returns in a panic and throws them at her as he bolts past on his way into the kitchen.)*

KLAUS. Here!

(While **KLAUS** *is in the kitchen, unseen by the audience, he puts on a chef's hat, apron and bright yellow rubber gloves used for washing dishes. He also grabs a large soup ladle – goodness knows what he plans to do with this!)*

INGRID. *(she catches the sheets)* What am I supposed to do with these? Tie them together and climb out the window? OWWWWWWW… OHHHHHHHHH! EEERRERREEEE!

KLAUS. *(from the kitchen)* I'll call the Tomassos! I saw them come back to the house with Sister Mary Gertrude! Mr. Tomasso smashed up his car.

*(***INGRID** *covers herself from her neck to her feet with the sheets.)*

INGRID. Oh no! How? *(She grimaces with pain and closes her eyes.)*

KLAUS. He slid into a tree when he tried to park in the driveway.

INGRID. *(Eyes closed, managing her pain.)* Was anyone hurt?

KLAUS. Just the car, I think. They were all arguing coming into the house so they must be all right. *(***KLAUS** *runs out of the kitchen, dressed in chef's hat, apron and yellow dish washing gloves and carrying the large soup ladle – he runs to the telephone and dials.* **INGRID** *on floor with eyes closed, breathing through her contractions, does not see him but the audience now does. He speaks into the phone in a panic.)* Mr. Tomasso! I'm sorry to call so late! Ingrid is in labor! My car won't start and the ambulance won't come because of the weather. Yes, could you please send Mrs. Tomasso and Sister Mary Gertrude? I am going to need their help.

INGRID. *(eyes closed, panting)* Oh Klaus! Not Sister Mary Gertrude. Just shoot me now.

KLAUS. *(into the telephone)* Yes, thank you, towels would be great. And, whatever else they can think of to bring.

INGRID. *(She opens her eyes and sees the bizarre way in which Klaus is dressed in chef's hat, apron and latex dishwashing gloves.)* Klaus! For Pete's sake! What are you planning to deliver? A turkey???

KLAUS. The hospital would have surgical garments! I am trying to improvise!

INGRID. OWWWWWWW.   OHHHHHHHHHHHHH! Here we go.

KLAUS. Okay, okay. I'm ready. I grew up next door to a hog farm in Germany. I saw this all the time. I can do this. I can do this. I can do this.

(He kneels or sits crossed legged on the floor in front of her feet and covers his head with the sheets. We see **INGRID***'s head at the one end and her feet and* **KLAUS***'s body at the other end. The majority of* **INGRID***'s body (knees bent with feet on the floor) and* **KLAUS***'s head (donned by the Chef's hat) and shoulders are covered by the sheets.)*

INGRID. Klaus. I…I have something to tell you.

KLAUS. *(Utterly distracted, with head under the sheets at her feet/ between her sheet-covered legs/knees)* Not now, sweetheart. I'm busy.

INGRID. Klaus, I've had a wonderful time these last few months. I don't know what is going to happen now. But, if it's what I think it is, I just want to say, I'm sorry. If I've been withdrawn or in any way indifferent to you…I just want to say that …I am sorry.

KLAUS. *(***KLAUS***'s head pops out from under the sheets to speak.)* You know, we haven't…well…you know…for months now. I was afraid you may have stopped loving me.

INGRID. Oh, Klaus, I just couldn't. I could not do that to Ingrid or you or Gr *(she is about to say Greg but instead says)* the baby. I love the baby too much. So, I thought it would be best to not…well…you know.

KLAUS. I can't say as though I do know. But, I'll try my best to understand. Later. Right now, I'm a little distracted. *(He pops his head back under the sheets at her feet as she has a major contraction, after which all the lights go out.)*

INGRID. ARRGGGHHHHHHHHHHHHHHHHHH! *(the lights go dark almost to a blackout. There can be a spotlight on INGRID on the floor.)* Klaus! Klaus! The power went out! We have no lights! How are you going to delivery the baby with no lights?

KLAUS. *(head popping out from under the sheets to speak)* We have candles. And flashlights. We'll manage. We can do this! I can do this!!!! *(He jumps up in a frenzy and runs into the kitchen to get a candle.)*

INGRID. ARRGGGGGGHHHHHHHHHHHHHHH!!!!!!! Klaus!!!! ARRRGGGGHHHHHHHHH!!!!!! Klaus!

KLAUS. You're doing fine. Just breathe. *(He scurries back into the living area and hands her a battery operated multi-color/changing window candle, turned on.)* I'll get a flashlight. *(He runs to the bedroom to get flashlight.)*

INGRID. *(On floor, holding up the window candle as if she were the Statue of Liberty)* Klaus, there is one more thing I need to tell you.

KLAUS. *(from bedroom)* Just a minute.

INGRID. IT'S IMPORTANT!!!!!!!!

(KLAUS rushes back with the flashlight, turned on)

KLAUS. What? What?

INGRID. Two things really. One: We must name this baby Gregory. No arguments! Gregory Klaus Wagner!

KLAUS. Okay. All right. Whatever you want! Gregory Klaus Wagner! If it's a girl, we'll name her Gregory Klaus Wagner! She'll blame you, not me. *(He kneels back down and puts his head under the sheets, holding the flashlight under the sheet.)*

INGRID. The next thing is even more important. Klaus! Klaus! ARE YOU LISTENING?????

KLAUS. *(His head pops out from under the sheets to speak.)* Yes! I am listening! I am listening! In between seeing our baby's head crowning, I'm LISTENING! *(KLAUS pops back under the sheets with flashlight and large kitchen serving spoon)*

INGRID. ARRGGGGHHHHHHH! Klaus! Listen to me! We must never go sailing!

KLAUS. *(head popping out from under sheets to speak)* What????

INGRID. You heard me! Repeat what I said!

KLAUS. We must never go sailing. Why?

INGRID. Never mind why! That's not important! What is important is that I never want to step foot on a boat with you!!!!! We are to never go on a boat! Will you remember that?

KLAUS. I promise you, I will never forget that we are never to go sailing! And, I promise you, I will never forget this night for as long as I live! *(He dives back under the sheets with ladle and flashlight)*

INGRID. Good! ARRGGGGHHHHHH!!!!!!

(We hear the loud cries of a newborn baby then...)

(Blackout/Curtain)

(lights, candle and flashlight out)

Scene 3

(The same. November 1st "real" time.)

(At Rise: ASHLEY is asleep, moaning on the sofa. She wears a robe, sweat pants and the night gown she originally wore before entering the wormhole. It is morning and the lights are up.)

ASHLEY. *(groaning and moaning but asleep)* OHHHHHHHH. ARRRRGGGGHHH. My stomach. It hurts! I'm not ready to be a mother. This isn't supposed to happen this way. *(more groaning and moaning)*

(HILDE and GERTIE bang on the door.)

HILDE. Are you all right in there?

(more moaning and groaning from ASHLEY)

GERTIE. What's all the commotion? *(to HILDE)* I saw Gregory leave for his appointment! What do you suppose she is doing in there all by herself? Hrmmmmph. I bet she's got one of those *battery operated gadgets!* She's just the sort who would, you know!

HILDE. You behave! I think she's sick. *(calling through the door)* Are you sick, honey?

ASHLEY. *(more groaning)* My stomach. Be careful with the baby! Don't drop him!

HILDE. I'm going in. *(She opens the door and finds ASHLEY asleep having a nightmare on the sofa.)*

GERTIE. Did she say *baby?*

(GERTIE and HILDE stand behind the sofa and look down upon ASHLEY.)

HILDE. She's dreaming.

(ASHLEY moans some more and utters some intelligible words that may be mistaken for chicken caccitori or ravioli or lasagna or eggplant parmesan or spaghetti and meatballs or linguime, veal scallopini, cannolis.)

I wonder what about?

GERTIE. Sounds like an Italian smorgasbord.

HILDE. *(stage whisper)* Maybe she's dreaming about a vacation in Italy.

GERTIE. I still say she has a *brotchen in ofen*. She just won't admit it.

HILDE. I'm going to wake her. *(She starts to gently shake her awake but* **GERTIE** *abruptly slaps her arm away stopping her.)*

GERTIE. No! I want to hear what else she says!

MR. TOMASELLI. *(from offstage)* Hello? Fräuleins! Anybody home?

GERTIE. What's he doing here? There is no mail on Sunday!

HILDE. He asked me out to brunch. As a "thank you" for lunch yesterday.

GERTIE. Well you said "No" I hope!

HILDE. I did no such thing. I asked him to pick me up at eleven. *(She looks at her watch.)* And it's eleven on the dot. He's a mailman. He's punctual!

GERTIE. I can't believe you have a date with the letter carrier.

HILDE. Well I do. I have a brunch date, Gertie. And, I'm going to have fun!

MR. TOMASELLI. *(entering)* Hello Fräuleins!

HILDE & GERTIE. Shhhhhhhhhhh!

*(***MR. TOMASELLI*** joins the aunts behind the sofa.)*

MR. TOMASELLI. *(whispering)* What's going on?

HILDE. She's asleep.

(more moaning and unintelligle words from sleeping **ASHLEY** *on the sofa)*

MR. TOMASELLI. Are you going to watch her sleep for much longer? I didn't have my oatmeal this morning. I'm hungry.

HILDE. I'm going to wake her.

GERTIE. No, just a few more minutes. I want to see if she says it again.

MR. TOMASELLI. Says what again?

GERTIE. Something about a baby. I still say she's....

HILDE. *(cutting her off)* Stop that! She is NOT!

(GREG returns from appointment with Professor using the side/kitchen entrance. He is back to his "old pre-wormhole self", without a mustache, glasses, etc.)

GREG. Hi! What's going on?

(More moaning from ASHLEY "My Stomach" "My Stomach")

GREG. What's wrong with her?

GERTIE. We're not sure. We just got here. We heard her moaning so we let ourselves in. She's moaning about a ba...(She starts to say "baby" but HILDE elbows her in the ribs to shut her up)*

GREG. About what?

HILDE. Her stomach.

GREG. *(sitting on sofa beside ASHLEY, he gently shakes her)* Ash. Ash. Honey. Honey, wake up. *(she stirs)* That's right. C'mon. Honey, wake up. *(ASHLEY wakes up looks around, and sits up like a bolt.)*

ASHLEY. Where is he? *(looks around)* Where is he? Is he all right? I want to hold him.

GREG. Where is who, honey?

ASHLEY. Gregory! Where is he? I want him. Now! Did something bad happen? Oh no. Is he all right?

GREG. Who?

ASHLEY. Gregory!

GREG. What?

ASHLEY. I want Gregory! Right now!

GREG. Honey, I'm right here.

ASHLEY. *(coming out of her dream or wormhole or whatever phenomenon she just experienced)* GREGORY? Greg? Is that you? *(She touches his face.)*

GREG. Of course it's me, honey. Who else would I be?

ASHLEY. I...I'm back? We're home? I'M BACK! Yes! It worked! It worked! *(She throws her arms around* **GREG.***)*

GREG. Calm down. I think you had a bad dream.

ASHLEY. Oh, no. No, I experienced a time and space phenomenon! It was like nothing that's ever happened to me before. The clock! All because of the clock!

GREG. The clock? What clock?

ASHLEY. That one! The cuckoo! It has a wormhole!

GREG. It is very old. I guess a worm could have worked a hole in it somewhere.

ASHLEY. No! Not that kind of wormhole. The scientific kind. The space and time kind!

GREG. Honey, you had a bad dream. It's over now.

ASHLEY. No! Greg, I'm telling you. I traveled back in time! I met your parents!

GREG. My parents?

ASHLEY. I knew your father! I was...*(she stops knowing what she would say is too outrageous for words)* I was very close with your mother.

GREG. And, how well did you know my father?

ASHLEY. *(blurting it out)* I NEVER SLEPT WITH HIM! I SWEAR!!!!!

GREG. *(laughing)* I should hope not!

ASHLEY. And, I met the Tomassos!

GREG. Who?

ASHLEY. Mr. and Mrs. Tomasso. The old Italian couple who sold their house to your parents. Mrs. Tomasso threw me a baby shower.

GREG. You had a baby?

GERTIE. I knew it! Now it comes out. The *kind* is probably five years old.

ASHLEY. No. No. I meant to say, they threw your mother a baby shower. I was there, that's all.

GREG. That's a whopper of a wormhole, Ash. Then what happened?

ASHLEY. I, ah. I turned the clock ahead. The cuckoo clock. And, here I am. I'm back. I was gone for…five months or so.

GREG. Five whole months? (*He stage whispers in her ear but doesn't really care who else hears.*) No wonder I'm so horny.

ASHLEY. What day is today?

MR. TOMASELLI. (*trying to be helpful*) Today is Sunday, November first. No mail delivery on Sundays!

ASHLEY. And, Greg! I warned your father! I did!

GREG. Warned him about what?

ASHLEY. I begged him! I begged him to never take me..I mean, never to take your mother, Ingrid, sailing. I told him to never take her on a boat. Oh, Greg. He must not have listened. I'm so sorry. Unless…unless…(*in earnest*) Greg, are your parents…still alive?

GREG. No, honey. I told you, my parents died in a boating accident. When I was a baby.

(**HILDE** *looks at* **GERTIE**. **GERTIE** *looks at* **HILDE**. *They both look down sheepishly at their feet, uneasy and squeamish at having perpetuated a lie for many years*)

GREG. What? What is it?

HILDE. Well…that's not exactly what happened.

GREG. What do you mean that's not exactly what happened? My parents had a boating accident. They were lost at sea.

GERTIE. Well…yes. And no.

GREG. All these years you told me that…

HILDE. We know what we told you.

GREG. Then what happened to them?

GERTIE. They were, ah, lost at sea. That much is true. But, they never went sailing.

GREG. Then why did you tell me they did?

GERTIE. Because they were supposed to go. But they didn't.

GREG. Why not?

HILDE. Your father wanted to charter a boat for their anniversary. But then he remembered something your mother made him promise. To never take her sailing. She did not want to get on a boat.

ASHLEY. I know! I was there when she said that. She warned him!

GREG. I thought you said you warned him.

ASHLEY. We both warned him. Your mother and I.

GERTIE. Well, somebody sure should have warned him about going rock climbing.

GREG. *Rock climbing?*

HILDE. Instead of sailing they went rock climbing.

GERTIE. They were a very athletic couple.

GREG. Why did you tell me they had a boating accident?

HILDE. Because what actually happened to them would have given you nightmares.

GERTIE. You were too little to know.

GREG. *(in disbelief)* What? What happened to them????

HILDE. They fell off a mountain or a bluff, whatever you call it. Overlooking the sea. They were tethered together. You see, there was an earthquake. A small tremor. It triggered a partial avalanche. The rock they were climbing gave way and they tumbled off right into the sea just as a yacht was pulling into the dock and it just creamed them. There was nothing much left of them.

GERTIE. *(matter of factly)* Fish food.

GREG. Where did this happen?

HILDE. Monte Carlo.

GREG. Monte Carlo???? They went to Monte Carlo to go rock climbing for the weekend?

HILDE. Well, it was a long weekend.

GERTIE. Fourteen days.

GREG. And they left me behind all that time with the old Italian couple downstairs?

ASHLEY. Mr. and Mrs. Tomasso! I met them! They were wonderful to us. That is, to your father and mother. They didn't really want to move to Florida but they had already put a deposit on a retirement condominium.

(GERTIE and HILDE look sheepishly at each other again and squirm… another piece of fiction is about to be exposed.)

GREG. What now???????

HILDE. Uh…the old Italian couple… Their name wasn't Tomasso. It was Taccarrelli…

GERTIE. …and Torregrossa.

ASHLEY. No! Mr. and. Mrs. Tomasso! I met them!

HILDE. Actually, it was Jimmy Taccarrelli.

GERTIE. And Joey Torregrossa.

HILDE. A nice older…

GERTIE. …couple of flaming homosexuals. They couldn't wait to sell the place to your parents so they could move down to South Beach. Wanted to retire where the action is!

GREG. *(crushed with disbelief)* My entire life has been a lie.

GERTIE. *(grabbing him by the earlobe and pulling him center stage, admonishing)* Your whole life has been every wonderful thing you remember it to be. We just embellished on a couple of details here and there that we felt you didn't really need to know. The truth is, kiddo, the two of us love you very much. And if you don't know that by now, you're a complete…

HILDE. *Dummkopf!*

ASHLEY. *(doubles over)* Oh. Oh, my stomach.

MR. TOMASELLI. I think I know what your problem is.

ASHLEY. *(emphatically)* I'm *not* pregnant!

MR. TOMASELLI. No, no! I didn't think you were. Your problem is that you just need a little Pepto Bismol. I have some in my car. I'll go get it. I also have Tums, Zantac, Alka Seltzer and Maalox.

GREG. Thanks, Mr. Tomaselli.

ASHLEY. Why do you carry all that medicine around with you, Mr. Tomaselli?

TOMASELLI. Er...I..ah...

GERTIE. Go ahead. You may as well confess. I suspected as much. *(to* **HILDE***)* But, if I told you, you'd never believe me.

HILDE. What?

GERTIE. Your Italian boyfriend here doesn't like your German cooking so much after all. *(to* **TOMASELLI***)* Do you?

*(***MR. TOMASELLI** *looks sheepishly down at his feet.)*

HILDE. Is that so, Lorenzo? You do not care for my cooking?

TOMASELLI. Well, to be honest, it is a bit rich for my digestive system. I have a wee bit of an ulcer. It tends to aggravate it. Once or twice your schnitzel even caused me to have a nightmare!

HILDE. Then why do you eat it with such enthusiasm every time you come to drop off the mail?

ASHLEY. Isn't it obvious, Tante Hilde?

HILDE. Not to me. I would never eat food I didn't like.

MR. TOMASELLI. I pretend to eat your food with gusto because I know how much you like to prepare it for me. And, because I so enjoy spending my lunch hours with you.

*(***GREG** *goes to window and looks out.)*

GREG. Hey! It's snowing outside. Do you ever remember it snowing on November first? It's actually coming down pretty hard. The streets are covered.

GERTIE. So, there! How do you like that, Hilde? You have a boyfriend all right! But, he doesn't like your German cooking! You'll have to learn how to make lasagna, Italian meat balls, Italian wedding soup and veal scaloppini. What do think of that?

HILDE. *(Hilde looks at* **GERTIE***)* I think... *(then she looks to* **GREG** *and* **ASHLEY***)* I think... *(then she turns to* **MR. TOMASELLI***)* I think...*(then to audience, after a thoughtful beat, and with conviction!)* That's a *Crock of Schnitzel!*

(Blackout/Curtain)

END OF PLAY

AUTHOR'S NOTE ABOUT THE CURTAIN CALL

The actors portraying Hilde, Gertie and Tomaselli should come out for their curtain calls pulling suitcases, holding cameras, take their bows and point to each other and to the audience and take pictures. The curtain call should suggest that the Aunts and Mr. Tomaselli have just arrived at the airport to visit Greg and Ashley in the Galapagos Islands where Greg has been working at the Conservatory with his Professor. The actor portraying Greg should then come out for his bow wearing a baseball cap, sunglasses and binoculars and give a big welcome hug to the Aunts and shake Mr. Tomaselli's hand. While all this is going on, Ashley should strap back on her pregnant belly and come out for her bow wearing a maternity shirt with a hat and sunglasses. When the aunts see Ashley they rush to her and hug her and pat her pregnant belly. Tante Gertie's premonition has come true! Hilde and Gertie will have a "wee wee wunderkind" to overprotect and spoil after all! And, they could not be happier. Ashley can then admire Tante Hilde's new "engagement ring" (from Mr. Tomaselli, of course.) They then can point to the audience through the binoculars as if to suggest they are looking at exotic wildlife in the Galapagos. And, join hands for a final group bow. The curtain call should suggest that the entire group is now in the Galapagos, and that Hilde and Gertie have overcome their fear of flying – or at least – have sufficiently medicated themselves to take the trip. And, they are one happy (though one slightly dysfunctional) family. The very best kind! (bpw)

ENGLISH TRANSLATION OF GERMAN WORDS AND PHRASES FOUND IN *A CROCK OF SCHNITZEL*

German Word or Phrase	English Translation
Aber ja!	Yes, of course!
Ach du lieber!	Oh, for the love of (or synonym for "good grief!")
Anwalt	Lawyer
Beischlafen	Have sexual intercourse
Bitte akzeptieren sie meine entschuldigung	Please accept my apology
Brötchen in ofen	Bun in the oven
Büstenhalter	Brassiere
Dummkopf	Dimwit/Fool
Fräu	Married woman
Fräuleins	Unmarried woman/Miss
Gern geschehen	My pleasure
Ich bin sicher sie ist	I am sure she is
Jawohl	Yes
Jungfrau	Virgin
Kind	Child
Liebeswerben	Love making
Liebchen	Term of endearment (honey)
Meine gute	My good or my goodness
Mein Schwester ist en idiot.	My sister is an idiot
Offnen sie das packet	Open the package
Oma	Grandmother
Opa	Grandfather
Scheidung	Divorce
Schlichtheit	Chastity
Um Gottes Willen!	For Heaven's Sake!
Unter kliedung	Underwear
Tante	Aunt
Teufelskerl	Little devil of a fellow
Vegetarier	Vegetarian
Verfetten	Become obese
Wunderbar	Wonderful
Wunderkind	Wonderful child/ child prodigy
Zehn minuten	Ten minutes

PROPERTY LIST

Cuckoo clock, preferably authentic and old (does not need to be in working order)

Note affixed to clock with warning "not to touch dial"

Remote control for television (note: the "high tech television" referenced by Hilde can be in the audience, on the "fourth wall" - not a stage prop")

Feather duster

Bucket with toilet brush/cleaning supplies/mop

Baking pan (of schnitzel) covered with foil for Hilde to put in freezer

Framed photograph of Ingrid and Klaus

Newspaper for Klaus to make first entrance

Telephone Book

Telephone

Shipping box for cuckoo clock

Rent check for Klaus to hand to Mr. Tomasso

Bed sheets (2) (can be single sized flat sheets)

Flashlight

Battery operated window candle (preferably one that changes color)

Chef's hat

Chef's apron (with bib) – frilly, colorful and feminine

Colorful rubber gloves (yellow or blue) for washing dishes/cleaning

Large Soup Ladle

Snow shovel

Ashley and Greg are "coming home" so both should have large backpacks or some sort of travel gear as they make their first "kissing and groping" entrance during which they shed the excess outer clothing and travel gear in the heated frenzy.

Optional laptop case or back pack for Greg to make last entrance from meeting with Professor.

Optional props/costume items for "family reunion in the Galapagos" curtain call:

Cameras

Suitcases

Pill bottle (from which Gertie and Hilde can help themselves after the plane ride)

Sunglass/sun hats/sandals

Hilde's engagement ring

.

COSTUME SUGGESTIONS

Act I, Scene I

    HILDE and **GERTIE** – every day "around the house" wear/ house cleaning attire

    GREG and **ASHLEY** – jeans, jackets, hats, scarves, casual "travel" clothing. Sneakers or boots as deemed appropriate by the director.

    MR. TOMASELLI – postman uniform

Act I, Scene II

    ASHLEY/INGRID - baby doll nightie under sweat pants, flannel shirt, slight padding around abdomen as if to suggest that the coveted "skinny jeans" don't quite zip anymore

    GREG – jeans, T-shirt or long sleeve shirt, sneakers

    KLAUS – glasses, moustache, hair combed differently, blazer, nice shirt, slacks and shoes

    MR. TOMASSO – cardigan sweater with button down shirt, slacks, loafers or other casual shoes, glasses

    MRS. TOMASSO – skirt and blouse with hair worn differently than in Scene 1

    SISTER MARY GERTRUDE – nun's habit

Act II, Scene I

    ASHLEY/INGRID – Same as Act I, Scene II but with over-coat/jacket on top of shirt and sweat pants for return from hospital

    KLAUS – Same as Act I, Scene II but with jacket for return from hospital

Act II, Scene II

    INGRID – maternity clothing with an "easy on/easy off" Velcro-enabled pregnancy suit underneath (she's nine months pregnant and as big as a barn)

    KLAUS – overcoat, hat, gloves, sweater, slacks, boots

    MR. TOMASSO – overcoat, hat, gloves, sweater, slacks, boots

    MRS. TOMASSO – sweater, skirt and shoes (baby shower attire)

    SISTER MARY GERTRUDE – nun's habit and black shawl or cloak

Act II, Scene III

ASHLEY – same as Act I Scene II

GREG - sweatshirt or jacket over slacks or jeans and sneakers or boots

HILDE – nice sweater, slacks and shoes for her brunch date with Mr. Tomaselli

GERTIE – around-the-house attire

MR. TOMASELLI – nice sweater, slacks and shoes for his date with Hilde

SET DESIGN/FURNISHING SUGGESTIONS

Greg's upstairs apartment should have a door leading to the downstairs/main part of the house. It should also have a separate outside/side door entrance from which there is a small landing/deck and outside stairs. There is an off-stage kitchen area and on-stage doors leading to to a bedroom and bathroom – or a hallway that leads to a bathroom and bedroom.

Simple furnishings should include the following:

Sofa or love seat,

Two chairs

A small dinette set

A telephone table (with phone)

Throw rug

The furniture should not be new as it needs to double as that which belonged to Greg's parents, Klaus and Ingrid.

Also by
Barbara Pease Weber...

Delval Divas

Hogwash

Seniors of the Sahara

OTHER TITLES AVAILABLE FROM BAKER'S PLAYS

SENIORS OF THE SAHARA

Barbara Pease Weber

Romantic Comedy / 3-4m, 4f

Sylvia Goldberg, a respectable retired New Jersey school teacher, brings home more than just souvenirs upon returning from her grandson's wedding in Israel. Sylvie's troubles begin when she realizes that the old teapot she purchased at an outdoor market is actually a priceless relic containing a geriatric genie "Eugene" with a bad back and a penchant for vodka and V8. Keeping Eugene a secret from her three best friends, Mabel, Thelma and Fannie, proves to be nearly as difficult as protecting herself from Eugene's former master who follows Sylvie home and threatens her at knifepoint. Be careful what you wish for, Sylvie Goldberg! You never know, it might come true. *Seniors of the Sahara* is a magical romantic comedy for seniors and "juniors" of all ages.

"*Seniors of the Sahara* is a comedy for the whole family"
– *Montgomery Newspapers*

"There are plenty of laughs to be had"
– *The Review*

"An imaginative piece"
– *Chestnut Hill Local*

SAMUEL FRENCH STAFF

Nate Collins
President

Ken Dingledine
Director of Operations,
Vice President

Bruce Lazarus
Executive Director,
General Counsel

Rita Maté
Director of Finance

ACCOUNTING

Lori Thimsen | Director of Licensing Compliance
Nehal Kumar | Senior Accounting Associate
Josephine Messina | Accounts Payable
Helena Mezzina | Royalty Administration
Joe Garner | Royalty Administration
Jessica Zheng | Accounts Receivable
Andy Lian | Accounts Receivable
Zoe Qiu | Accounts Receivable
Charlie Sou | Accounting Associate
Joann Mannello | Orders Administrator

BUSINESS AFFAIRS

Lysna Marzani | Director of Business Affairs
Kathryn McCumber | Business Administrator

CUSTOMER SERVICE AND LICENSING

Brad Lohrenz | Director of Licensing Development
Fred Schnitzer | Business Development Manager
Laura Lindson | Licensing Services Manager
Kim Rogers | Professional Licensing Associate
Matthew Akers | Amateur Licensing Associate
Ashley Byrne | Amateur Licensing Associate
Glenn Halcomb | Amateur Licensing Associate
Derek Hassler | Amateur Licensing Associate
Jennifer Carter | Amateur Licensing Associate
Kelly McCready | Amateur Licensing Associate
Annette Storckman | Amateur Licensing Associate
Chris Lonstrup | Outgoing Information Specialist

EDITORIAL AND PUBLICATIONS

Amy Rose Marsh | Literary Manager
Ben Coleman | Editorial Associate
Gene Sweeney | Graphic Designer
David Geer | Publications Supervisor
Charlyn Brea | Publications Associate
Tyler Mullen | Publications Associate

MARKETING

Abbie Van Nostrand | Director of Corporate
Communications
Ryan Pointer | Marketing Manager
Courtney Kochuba | Marketing Associate

OPERATIONS

Joe Ferreira | Product Development Manager
Casey McLain | Operations Supervisor
Danielle Heckman | Office Coordinator, Reception

SAMUEL FRENCH BOOKSHOP (LOS ANGELES)

Joyce Mehess | Bookstore Manager
Cory DeLair | Bookstore Buyer
Jennifer Palumbo | Customer Service Associate
Sonya Wallace | Bookstore Associate
Tim Coultas | Bookstore Associate
Monté Patterson | Bookstore Associate
Robin Hushbeck | Bookstore Associate
Alfred Contreras | Shipping & Receiving

LONDON OFFICE

Felicity Barks | Rights & Contracts Associate
Steve Blacker | Bookshop Associate
David Bray | Customer Services Associate
Zena Choi | Professional Licensing Associate
Robert Cooke | Assistant Buyer
Stephanie Dawson | Amateur Licensing Associate
Simon Ellison | Retail Sales Manager
Jason Felix | Royalty Administration
Susan Griffiths | Amateur Licensing Associate
Robert Hamilton | Amateur Licensing Associate
Lucy Hume | Publications Manager
Nasir Khan | Management Accountant
Simon Magniti | Royalty Administration
Louise Mappley | Amateur Licensing Associate
James Nicolau | Despatch Associate
Martin Phillips | Librarian
Zubayed Rahman | Despatch Associate
Steve Sanderson | Royalty Administration Supervisor
Douglas Schatz | Acting Executive Director
Roger Sheppard | I.T. Manager
Geoffrey Skinner | Company Accountant
Peter Smith | Amateur Licensing Associate
Garry Spratley | Customer Service Manager
David Webster | UK Operations Director

SAMUELFRENCH.COM
SAMUELFRENCH-LONDON.CO.UK